THE GUN WAS OUT AND RANGE WAR BEGAN

Clint set his sights dead on the ambusher, who was waiting for his prey. He thought of giving the man warning, but decided against it. An ambusher was worse than a vicious jackal. He deserved no mercy.

The ambusher was unaware that he, too, was a target. Clint's breath stopped and he squeezed the trigger. The echo ricocheted through the clean air. The ambusher jumped once and never moved again.

One man down. But how many more lurked in the shadows? No matter! Clint vowed to get them all.

Ernest Haycox

Ⓢ Signet Brand Western

SIGNET Westerns by Ernest Haycox

Dead Man Range

(Formerly titled *Clint*)

by ERNEST HAYCOX

A SIGNET BOOK

NEW AMERICAN LIBRARY

TIMES MIRROR

SIGNET TRADEMARK REG. U.S. PAT. OFF. AND FOREIGN COUNTRIES
REGISTERED TRADEMARK——MARCA REGISTRADA
HECHO EN CHICAGO, U.S.A.

SIGNET, SIGNET CLASSICS, MENTOR, PLUME AND MERIDIAN BOOKS
are published by The New American Library, Inc.,
1301 Avenue of the Americas, New York, New York 10019

FIRST PRINTING, MAY, 1975

1 2 3 4 5 6 7 8 9

PRINTED IN THE UNITED STATES OF AMERICA

Chapter ONE

The sprawling, haze-dimmed outline of Angels, Casa-bella County's official seat and only town, had been in front of Clint Charterhouse all during the last five miles riding across the undulating prairie. And because many days and weeks of lonely traveling had taught this tall, hazel-eyed man the value of keeping his mind always occupied he had been speculating on the nature of this remote and isolated place. Experience told him it would be just another double row of sun-baked, paint-peeled buildings with a dusty sweltering street between; and since it was just past noon the citizens would be indoors dawdling. Clint Charterhouse, footloose and fancy free, had entered into and departed from a hundred such habitations of man and found none of them different.

But as he checked his horse at the very limits of Angels, he discovered all his guesses wrong. This town was different and, with a quick interest breaking through the long saddle drowse, he swept the scene. There indeed lay the double row of paint-peeled buildings, perhaps fifteen on a side, and along the fronts of all ran second story porches that made of each sidewalk a long and shaded gallery. But Angels itself was far from being asleep on this sultry, droning day. The town was full of men. A particular knot of them stood in front of an expansive porch at the far end; lesser groups were by the stable, the saloons, the blacksmith's yawning door. Honest hammer strokes clanged off an anvil; horses rubbed sides at the racks; more riders coursed rapidly into Angels from the far end; and more men waddled across the plaza.

"Court day?" Clint Charterhouse asked himself. "No, it's the wrong time of the year. Here it is Monday in the middle of roundup season and by every rule of the range

5

this joint ought to be dead as a door nail." His hazel glance narrowed down the street, more closely studying those indolent groups of men. "Might be just my imagination, or do I sort of see them square off against each other, watchful-like? Heard somewhere Casabella took its politics serious—and continuous. For a practically honest man looking for practically honest toil this ain't so good. I'd hate to dab a rope on trouble." But as he said it he smiled. White teeth flashed against a bronzed skin, and a flare of high-humored excitement broke the severity of his eyes.

As he was observing, so was he being observed. He saw men swing in his direction and stand waiting. And since it was almost as bad taste to stand on the edge of a strange town and peer in as it was to stand outside a strange window and eavesdrop, he spoke gently to the horse and proceeded casually forward. If Angels this day contained two factions—and the impression that such was the case grew more strangely pronounced in Clint Charterhouse's shrewd head—then his entry was somewhat ticklish, for any stray or innocent act might be taken as an indication of his own politics. If he racked his horse on either side he might be involuntarily swearing himself into partisanship with one group. Studying the situation quickly he decided safety lay in putting up his horse at the only visible stable on the street and so he veered in that direction, conscious that he was being scanned by fifty pairs of eyes.

For that matter horse and rider were worth a second glance. The horse, a true representative of the cowpony—the toughest, staunchest breed in the world for the work it performs—was a glistening coal-black and so largely proportioned that it escaped the stubby, end-for-end look of the average range product. By some reversion of nature the fine Arab blood of its ancestors flared strongly in carriage and muscle. Upon its back rested a magnificent square-skirted saddle stamped with an oak leaf pattern and mounted with silver ornaments.

As for Clint Charterhouse who sat so negligently in this leathered elegance no man in Angels could ever mistake him. Western born, Western raised, he carried the plain print of the land on him. In a country that matured all animate things swiftly, shot them to height yet pinched their girth, Clint Charterhouse followed the rule. There were few men he had to lift his head to, and his shadow on the ground was as slim as the rest. Yet it was not a disjointed slimness. In his flat sinews was a latent strength and in his carriage was a promise of sure and easy swiftness. He had his hat canted slightly to one side and the hot sunlight angled across a bold nose, rounding lips and a square chin. There was a leanness to his face, a clean cut of all features that fell just short of being gaunt. And he looked around at the street and the curious men with an easy gravity. He heard somebody's murmured "Who's Han'some?" but he elected not to take cognizance. Passing into the stable, he slipped saddle and gear to convenient pegs, left a few instructions with the hostler and turned out again, rolling a cigarette.

The business of building himself a cigarette was to screen a closer scrutiny of his surroundings. If ever a town was troubled with uncertainty and foreboding, Angels filled the bill. Peaceable men didn't stand around in the sultry heat like this; and peaceful men didn't labor so hard to feign indifference. The crowd on this side of the street seemed a little heavier than that on the other and a uniform brand was on most of the ponies over here—Box M.

"Must be an all-fired big outfit," he told himself, applying a match to his smoke. A pair of men slid casually into the stable behind him, at which Clint Charterhouse allowed himself a reasonable deduction. They were going to give his horse a closer and more thorough scrutiny. "Not that I blame them under the circumstances," he added. "Looks to me as if this was one of those cases where folks only believe what they see and maybe not all of that. But supposing I wasn't a harmless stranger—what could I be that would do 'em any damage? State official, hired gun artist? Doggoned if this don't grow interesting. Little Rollo had better watch his step."

There was a general stirring of men around him. Across the plaza the doors of a saloon swung to emit a pair of citizens who marched diagonally into the dusty area. One man was beyond middle age and massively scowling; the other was no older than Clint Charterhouse, yellow-haired and laughing. Together the two disappeared in the crowd at the far end of the town and thence inside the building. Perceptibly the interest of Angels shifted that way and more loitering fellows drifted off. But Clint Charterhouse looked at the saloon. It seemed common ground; parties from both sides were crowding through to drink and so he cruised casually across and presently was at a bar forty feet long, wedged between other thirsting gentry and hearing the swell of much talk.

"Make way, Lum," said a voice behind him. The man at his right elbow swung a swift glance over his shoulder and then edged off from the bar to admit a broad and closely coupled gentleman who regarded Clint Charterhouse with a blunt, direct interest. "Stranger to these parts, sir?"

"Call it so," replied Charterhouse, noncommittal. He was about to pour himself a drink when the heavy personage reached over and thrust the bottle away, lifting one finger to the barkeep. "My personal brand, Jim." He turned to Charterhouse again. "No offense. Make it a point to always greet strangers in my establishment. Nero Studd is the name, and pleased to meet you."

"Charterhouse is mine."

They shook gravely, Clint looking down slightly. Nero Studd wore a black serge suit that wrinkled at all his thick joints and a white shirt that needed changing. He was a swart man with one black cowlick curling upon a glistening forehead. Smoke-colored eyes sat far back in sockets overhung with bushing brows, and a nose, seemingly without cartilage, splayed against the upper lip. This irregularity of features conspired to give him the character of some barroom bruiser, which was only partly alleviated by the bluff cordiality he displayed. "Try a little of that liquor. On me. Charterhouse was the name? I knew some Charterhouses down on the Border."

Charterhouse drank with due deliberation. "Mighty potent after a long ride. I'm obliged to you, sir. I never knew anybody of my name in the region you mention."

The nearby loiters were listening closely; the hum of talk had definitely subsided. Nero Studd rubbed his oil-damp cheeks. "Well, names don't always mean so much. Come to think, I rode once with another Charterhouse in Colorado."

"They say it is a nice state and sometimes cool," was Charterhouse's agreeable and vague response.

Studd's eyes kept lifting to Charterhouse's face and falling away. "Well, consider this your stamping ground when in Angels. If there's anything I can ever do, call on me." He waved aside an invitation to drink. "Thanks, but no. You'll understand if I imbibed my own poison I'd be under the tables in no time."

"Obliged for the offer," said Charterhouse. "I will remember—" He stopped short as a robust war-whoop diverted his attention toward the door. In staggered a brawny, grinning young fellow clasping an enormous slab of granite rock against his chest. He left it fall crashing to the floor and stepped back to drench the moisture from his face and chuckle admiringly at his own effort. "Now I got something you buzzards can sink your teeth in."

"You'll bust the hell out of my floor," said Nero Studd, not so cordially.

"Yeah? Well, I spend enough money in this dump to floor it with diamonds," replied the roly-poly young fellow. His eyes searched the room. "Now I want something to prop this monster up with. I'll show you a trick to grow hair on the chest." Going behind the bar, he serenely appropriated four fresh packs of playing cards and went back to the rock. Using the card packs as supports, he created a small space beneath the rock. Sitting on his haunches, he slipped one broad paw into this space and looked about him with a sparkle of irrepressible humor. "Now observe what a man can do, my children."

He had the full attention of everybody. Somebody muttered, "Bet ten dollars that fool Heck Seastrom will fall flat on his south end." Young Seastrom only grinned and squared his enormous shoulders to the rock. His palm pressed up against the weight; Charterhouse saw all the rope-like muscles of the fellow's chest, arms and neck stand out against a reddening skin. There was an enormous gust of breath. The rock rose by degrees, shoulder high and then soared overhead as Seastrom stood erect. Sweat poured down his cheeks but he was still grinning when he let the rock smash to the floor again. "Now . . . you . . . curly-tailed wolves!" he panted. "Try that on your big bazoo! Drinks on me—if any man boosts it!" He draped himself on the bar and stared fondly at the rock while fighting for wind.

"You cracked a board," stated Nero Studd, glumly. "Why don't you save some of that steam for honest labor?"

"We will now pray," jeered Heck Seastrom amiably. "Brother Studd will read the Bible lesson and lead the singing. Ain't that a stem-winder of a stunt? Who's a-going to try it? Don't be bashful."

One of the crowd kicked the rock tentatively and stepped back, but there were no takers. Somebody in the background murmured softly, "It ain't always a matter of muscles, Seastrom. There's other ways."

The remark hung strangely in the room, intensifying the silence. Clint Charterhouse felt more strongly the undercurrent of antagonism. Everybody stood still; faces ranked darkly in the shaded room, a sibilant breath sheered the sultry atmosphere, and then men shifted uneasily. Nero Studd's dark face turned slowly around the semicircle, deliberately blank.

"I was a-waiting for a crack like that," drawled young Heck Seastrom indolently. "In answer to which I will say there sure is plenty of other ways. Hiding behind the brush, for example, and taking pot shots. Was that the way you thought of, fella?"

Clint Charterhouse felt a pull of admiration for Seastrom's easy-going manner. The burly young puncher bubbled over with vital humor; and not even the threat of trouble could change him much. But Nero Studd suddenly shifted and broke the dangerous moment, speaking with a gruff jest. "Wait till Buck Manners comes around, Seastrom. He'll peg that trick of yours right off the bat."

"Will he?" challenged Seastrom. "Say, I figured out

this stunt with just him in mind. Blame near busted my
back finding a rock heavy enough, just to stop that particular gent. Wait and see."

"A month's pay he can lift it," offered Studd.

"Took," agreed Heck Seastrom. "I got something finally
which is sure a-going to frazzle him. If it don't, I'll be the
cross-eyed son of a cross-eyed father."

Traffic at the bar resumed and Nero Studd moved
through the room, passing a word here and there, occa-
sionally resting his heavy arm on some man's shoulder,
Clint Charterhouse let his attention follow this saloon pro-
prietor for quite a while; then he turned to a barkeep.
"Give me a pint of straight, uncut alcohol."

The barkeep was diverted out of his heavy indifference.
"Must be packing a big thirst," said he. But Charterhouse
paid for the pint and walked silently out of the place with
the bottle in his hand. Crossing the plaza, he went down
the stable alley to his horse and began to rub the alcohol
on the animal's back.

Over in front of the saloon a pair of men slouched
against a porch and watched him.

"Massaging that horse with good liquor," said one.

"Must like that horse," said the other, narrowing his
lids.

"Must be a real good horse," added the first. They ex-
changed solemn glances. Number One nodded slightly at
Number Two.

Chapter TWO

At the northeast corner of the plaza stood Madame LeSeur's house, which was all that Casabella could claim in the line of hotel, eating place and rendezvous for social affairs. Madame was a stout square woman with traces of former beauty, and a witty, sharp-tongued kindness. It was common belief that in earlier days she had been the toast of a dance hall in far off Deadwood, a belief she neither confirmed nor denied. Not that it mattered here, for Casabella implicitly believed anybody's past was his or her own affair. All it positively knew was that Madame LeSeur had drifted into Angels, built this ramshackle place with a three-sided porch, divided the second story into innumerable cubicles for sleeping purposes, and arranged the downstairs into kitchen, dining room and a vast lobby with crystal chandeliers.

According to Madame's own statement, the bedrooms were of two kinds. Those large enough for a horse to turn around in were "double" and worth fifty cents the sleep. Those too narrow to pass the horse-turning test were "singles" at two bits the throw. Many a puncher, whose last alcoholic remembrance had been of slumping into the watering trough of the plaza, had wakened in one of Madame's rooms, charitably housed by her orders. To all such gentlemen's embarrassed thanks she invariably retorted that business was business and she had to fill up her house one way or another; and the bill would be a quarter-dollar, if you please, with no charge for cartage.

The lobby had been the scene of famous events, and today another was in the making. For in this lobby were gathered men, ranchers and townsmen, bent on threshing out a question never yet solved in Casabella—the question of peace.

Some were seated at the big round table. Buck Manners was in his chair, seesawing it on the back legs. Buck was the slim and smiling man Clint Charterhouse had seen crossing the plaza a few minutes earlier. He was seated and still showed a good-natured expression, even though the single flip of a phrase threatened to turn the town into a blaze of war. Sheriff Drop Wolfert was seated, too. His hands were lying flat on the table's surface, and his narrowed, sulky eyes were following around from man to man. Never amiable, his temper was further inflamed this afternoon from knowing that his authority was scornfully questioned and his motives doubted. Beef Graney sat next to the sheriff. Beef was a figure with a few dubious acres of range and a small scattering of stock. He was slyly keeping his eyes down. There was no mistaking the ruddy bull-dog of a man who dominated the meeting. John Nickum was of the Western type that produced the great cattle kings. Even now when the middle fifties had fleshed up his big bones and shot his hair with gray, there still remained the chill blue directness of his eyes that signaled relentless personal courage. Kindly, jovial, never forsaking a friend nor committing deliberate meanness, he possessed all the old baronial virtues.

His faults sprang from the same source. He had fought too hard in his life to forgive an enemy; to them he was ruthless. For him there was no middle ground, no mellowed tolerance. The qualities of the land itself were in him, and he could not change. He had seen good men fall and the lesson of their lives had stiffened his own rugged back. Piece by piece the great Box M had been wrung from his sweat and scheming; every step of the way he had been harried by the inevitable outlaws who snapped at his flanks. Blow for blow he had fought them without pity; now that his power was again being undermined he placed his back to the wall and roared his challenge.

"I am able to take care of my own quarrels," he said stiffly. "Nevertheless, I called you here to tell you and warn you that a pack of yellow hounds are building up their machine to wreck me. If they succeed, they will wreck you as well. I have cleaned up more than one magpie's nest in my time. I have the power still to do it."

"Fine talk," broke in Shander, another powerful rancher, pressing the words between his thin lips. "Since you are all wound up, suppose you mention some names? Who are these yellow dogs you mention?"

Old John Nickum's cold glance struck Shander. "I will take my own pleasure about that," said he.

"You take your own pleasure about a great many things," snapped Shander. "Too many things, if you ask me. Big as your damned outfit is, I am not afraid to stand up and speak my piece. Every man in this room understands who you are talking against. I'll just challenge you to state a few facts."

Both Sheriff Wolfert and Beef Graney lifted their heads in seeming assent, though Wolfert immediately covered his expression and tried to look neutral. Buck Manners laughed softly at him.

"So—facts?" muttered Nickum. "Here is one fact. Casabella's got a large floating population in the last few months that lifts no single hand in honest labor. You know what that means as well as I do. Take a count of Curly's outfit right now and you'd find it shot with the worst thieves and knife artists along the Border. I can go out to the street and point out six of his damned crew snoozing in the shade. I once was easy on him, and now he's the coldest leader of hired killers ever forked saddle in this country."

"Lay that to Casabella's salubrious climate," said Shander with evident sarcasm. "Can't deny any man's right to jump a county line for saftey, can you? Since when have you got so moral, anyhow? I'm prepared to say you've got riders in your own outfit whose pasts won't bear daylight. Who cares?"

"I will state another fact," went on old John Nickum, sweeping Shander's words aside. "On this very day we have a meeting, Angels is crowded with these last run of shad, armed to the teeth. What brings 'em here so suddenly?"

"Promise of excitement," retorted Shander. "What brought all your riders in?"

"Promise of excitement, eh? Promise of pay—promise of killings. Somebody is drumming up another mess of grief. I have cut my eye teeth, Shander. I know the signs as well as any man."

Shander's thin frame trembled. "By gosh, Nickum, I challenge you to name names. You are dragging a wide loop, and I'm warning it will snag you out of the saddle before long!"

"Oh, come," broke in Buck Manners easily. "This is getting rather stiff. Let's take another turn around the snubbing post and go slower. No need for you gentlemen to fight about it. Let's be reasonably calm."

But John Nickum ploughed doggedly ahead. He veered on Sheriff Wolfert. "Drop, you ain't blind, are you? You see Curly's riders floating through Angels, don't you. What in hell are you wearing a star for?"

Sheriff Wolfert grumbled morosely, "What of it? I got no bench warrants for any of Curly's men. I can't arrest nobody on plain suspicion. I got a warrant for Curly, but he's the only one of the gang I could legally arrest—if he showed his nose. Even so, what jury would hook Curly, or any of the rest? Man's got to use judgment in these things, Nickum. If I go throwing all suspicious folks in the calaboose, I'll be finding myself out in the mesquite some fine day."

"Great talk!" scouted Nickum. "You'd better put that star on your undershirt so folks won't see it. I'll tell you now, Wolfert, this is your last term in the office."

Wolfert flared up. "Oh, I don't know about that!" But both Graney and Shander looked at him so sharply that he stopped talking and sank back into the same morose silence. Everybody in the room caught that scene. Buck Manners' attention went up swiftly to the withdrawn Nero Studd and watched him momentarily. Nickum boomed on. "I have got something else to say to you, Wolfert. When my son was ambushed and killed in Red Draw, what did you do? You never moved out of your chair for two days. What have you done since? Nothing! Am I to believe you are making a tolerable effort to earn your money? I understand all about the petty graft you take and I am not kicking about it. But when you refuse to lift a hand to help Box M, I am forced to conclude that you got your fingers in a bigger kettle."

"Who said so?" yelled Wolfert, half rising. "Who give you license to call me thataway? Hell, I've worn my horses' shoes to paper in that damn country! If you want to know, I can't find a smell of a clue regarding who shot your son! I made an effort. Don't say I didn't. It's unfriendly for you to say I'm hooked up in any way with that affair. If I got to be blunt, Nickum, you talk to folks like they was school boys. It doesn't set straight. You hadn't ought to try to run other men's businesses for 'em. I'm able to handle my job."

"The great man," was Shander's cutting interjection, "doesn't forget he is the king-pin of Casabella. And the great man hasn't named any names yet."

But old John Nickum had straightened. He looked from the sheriff to Graney to Shander and on over to Nero Studd. "I am not crying about my loss," said he, even and cold. "I paid my just debts for fifty-eight years. I will continue to pay them—and to collect them. I was weaned on outlaws and crooked politics. I see what is going on here. I see another bright idea to hamstring Box M. It's been tried before by damned fools who think they got some original sure-thing racket. I say this, too. If those gentlemen who believe they can put me on the run want war, they shall have war!"

Buck Manners frowned. "Think it over. We ought to be able to settle this without recourse to shooting."

"Never mind, Buck," grunted Nickum. "I'm playing my hand."

"Not altogether," said Manners gently. "Remember the Manners family has strung along on your side for thirty good years and I expect to carry on my father's habits. I believe as you do, but I want to be sure we can't settle this peaceably."

"I haven't asked you to come in," was Nickum's short answer.

"No, but I'll be there with my outfit," Manners retorted.

Shander was grimly smiling. "After you, Alphonse. Virtue sure does drip over. I ain't heard any names mentioned yet."

"Were I you," said Manners coldly, "I'd take advantage of a pretty broad hint."

"Meaning what?" challenged Shander.

"Meaning this," said Nickum, taking up the thread. "The Box M draws a deadline today at its south limit, from Red Draw to Dead Man's Range. Any rider caught across that line will explain himself clearly or take the consequences."

"Answering for myself," said Shander, violently angered, "I never have had any desire to ride on your damned range and haven't now. Since you have been aiming your shots at me during this powwow, I want to say you can expect no further friendliness from myself or my men. I object to your insinuations. I hope Curly rustles you poor, curse you if I don't! Keep your riders off my range! I won't stand good for their safety from this day. And if you have any business with me, do it through a third party."

"I am glad to know," said Nickum formally, "you are willing to put yourself that far in the open. I detest a man concealing his state of mind."

"You're going too far, Nickum!"

"Meeting's adjourned," broke in Buck Manners and rose to place himself between the two men. "I guess we know where we stand. As for me, I string with Nickum any time, anywhere. I'd hate to see a range war, but I'll take care of my share of it when it comes."

"Listen," said Sheriff Wolfert, "you men are making it awful hard on me. If there's going to be ill will between outfits, there's sure to be gun play in Angels. Now I want this to be neutral ground all the time."

"I will state another fact," went on old John Nickum, "After this my men will come and go in parties, peaceably and without intent to quarrel."

Everybody waited for Shander to say as much. But he

was halfway to the door and only flung a short reply over his shoulder. "My riders can take care of themselves."

The meeting broke up. Nero Studd had already gone. Beef Graney overtook Shander and they left together. Wolfert remained seated, wrapped in gloom and only roused himself to shoot a covertly unpleasant glance at Nickum as the latter went out accompanied by Manners and Nickum's vinegary foreman, Driver Haggerty.

Nickum, striding massively between the two, looked all around the Plaza, the wrath still simmering in him. "Border jumpers, professional gunslingers, knife artists—the place is full of them. Look yonder by Nero Studd's joint. See those two fellows leaning against the porch post? Curley's men, ain't they?"

"Just so," agreed Buck Manners lazily.

"Shander's asking for trouble," muttered Nickum. "And he'll get it. He ain't smart enough for an old hand like me, not for a minute. He's the man who's drawing all the crooks together. He's making a play at me. He's got Wolfert obeying his orders. He's got Beef Graney, the poor fool, under his thumb. He's probably working hand in glove with that yellow-livered, greasy-fingered Nero Studd. Studd was always a cheap and crooked politician and always will be—sees everything, knows everything and draws the support of every outlaw in this country. And I'm betting Shander and Studd, between 'em, have got Curly lined up. A fine set of thieves—all pointing at me! Wolfert let the cat out of the bag when he same as said he'll be elected another term. Meaning he's got all the underhanded support."

Manners laughed. "I observed that Graney and Studd and Shander gave him some very dirty looks for making that break."

"You bet. Hand in glove." Nickum closed one big paw and struck at the air. "I am too old at this game to be beat now. I've licked harder men than they ever will be. They want war. I'll give 'em a bellyful of it, Buck! Who's that over there?"

He ducked his head at the ambling figure of Clint Charterhouse who, hat tilted rakishly against the burning sun, was crossing back to Studd's Saloon. Buck Manners stared intently. Driver Haggerty shifted his chew and spoke for the first time in an hour. "Stranger. Rode in a little while ago. Elegant horse with a strange brand and a heap expensive saddle."

"Strangers from now on had better declare themselves," grunted old John Nickum.

"Let's amble into Studd's for a drink," suggested Buck Manners. "Nero's probably got the man's personal history eight generations back."

"I wouldn't trust Nero behind my back in a crowded room," retorted Nickum. "Where's Sherry gone?"

"She's in Ortega's, buying a lot of notions," chuckled Manners, face lighting. Driver Haggerty's stringy countenance veered and covered Manners for a brief moment. Then all three of them passed into Nero Studd's.

Clint Charterhouse was standing beside Studd when the party entered and his attention instantly lighted on old John Nickum's imposing bulk. He knew a typical cattleman when he saw one and his reaction was to question the saloon keeper.

"Him?" replied Studd. "That's Nickum, Box M. Biggest outfit in Casabella. That homely mutt who looked like he's swallowed his tobacco is Haggerty, the foreman. Other man runs a range almost as big as Nickum's—Buck Manners. Inherited from his dad a year back."

"When I work," reflected Clint Charterhouse cheerfully, "I work for the top dog." He went forward, facing Nickum. The old ranchman stopped and stared truculently.

"Can you use another rider?" asked Charterhouse.

It was then that John Nickum committed an error. Almost always the soul of courtesy and usually the keenest judge of men, he was this afternoon in the grip of anger, stung by trouble and perplexed with the devious politics of the county. Thus he allowed himself to be gruff and unfriendly.

"I don't know you, sir."

Nettled by this obvious violation of the range's freemasonry, Charterhouse became gravely polite. "The same can be said, I reckon, of most men you hire. I didn't ask for partnership in Box M. I just asked for a job."

"So?" snapped Nickum, hackles rising. "Are you undertaking to dress me down, sir? I know my business well enough. And I'll repeat I don't know you. I have hired strangers and probably will again, but not at a time like this. At present drifters bear a bad name in Casabella. Where did you work last?"

"Since you don't intend to hire me," replied Charterhouse, increasingly formal, "I doubt if it's necessary to say. My apologies for taking your good time. It won't happen again."

The crowd in Studd's held its breath, waiting for the inevitable explosion to follow. Driver Haggerty's red little eyes glinted ominously, but Buck Manners relieved the tension with his infectious chuckle. "Damned if there isn't more powder in Angel's air today than ever I smelled before. After all, John, he's just looking for work. I don't see any horns on him." And he winked jovially at Charterhouse.

Once having taken his position, the old rancher would not back down. But his ingrained sense of propriety made a necessary concession. "If my talk seems unduly hard on your pride, sir, accept apologies. I am not hiring today."

"We will consider the incident closed," said Charterhouse levelly and turned his back on Nickum. Heck Seastrom bawled an order from the rear of the saloon. "Clear a space, you dudes! Hey, Manners, I got something that's a-going to stop you now. Take a look and bust out crying!"

A lane was made, revealing the irrepressible puncher standing affectionately over his immense rock. Manners laughed. "Still trying to cook up something to best me, huh? What do I do, lift it?"

"I got a month's pay salted which says you can't," stated Seastrom roundly. "Down on your heels, one hand, and she's got to go the full length of your arm overhead."

"Another month's pay I can," said Manners, crouching in front of the rock.

"Took!"

Manners threw off his hat, the curly yellow hair shining even in this dull light. The face grew astonishingly sober and hard, reminding Clint Charterhouse of a man slipping off a mask to reveal his true lineaments. Buck's palm rested beneath the rock; he put a tentative pressure against it, swayed on his heels once and said, "Hup!" mightily, body rising, weaving, and swinging around; the muscles of his slim neck went white, like taut cables, and the rock was poised overhead. He grinned again and cried, "Watch out!" Men ducked and the rock sailed down the room and went crashing through the floor.

The crowd yelled. "Now you've busted my floor!" cried Nero Studd angrily. But he was drowned out by Heck Seastrom who flung his hat down and stamped on it.

"Busted *your* floor? Hell, he's busted *me!* Two months' wages! I'll be working for Box M the rest of my natural life! I practiced six weeks on that trick!"

"Mebbe that's why you ain't no damn good when it comes to work," jeered somebody.

Buck Manners chuckled and walked to the end of the counter. "My turn now, Heck. Come down here and try another little test."

"Nossir, not me," protested Seastrom moodily. "I done had enough. I'm content to be second strongest man in this here county. Let it go like that."

Manners was in his element, a happy-go-lucky rowdy for the moment, with all the cares of his enormous holdings forgotten. "Anybody try. Come on." His glance arrived at Clint Charterhouse and stayed there. "You try, friend. I can't get any contest out of those buzzards any more. What's the fun of it if nobody will play in my back yard?"

"Why me?" countered Charterhouse, smiling slightly.

"Give him a play," urged Seastrom hopefully. The crowd closed in, interested in this stranger who so far had consistently refused to label himself. Charterhouse saw Manners eyeing him in cool calculation. Stepping around, he faced the yellow-haired cattleman across the bar. Manners had his right elbow on the bar, forearm raised; it was the old "muscling down" test, well known to Charterhouse, who extended his own right hand. They locked fingers and adjusted their elbows cagily. Manners grinned across at Charterhouse. "All set? Then—go!"

Charterhouse had braced his body against the bar, but the enormous power Manners threw into his forearm almost unbalanced him, even so. He locked his leg under a box of beer bottles, the cords of his wrist springing to the pressure. Manners had, in the first exertion of strength, pushed Charterhouse's arm slightly toward the bar, toward defeat. Charterhouse bowed his head and hurled his will into the protesting muscles. The cattleman's grip was like iron and he was using it to paralyze Charterhouse's finger nerves, crushing down. A runner of weakness began to deaden his arm, hot sweat started to his face; yet his wrist came upright again, and there strained on even terms. He lifted his head, catching the glances of those packed in the saloon. Manners was grinning through the strained lines of his cheeks but his eyes stared into Charterhouse's with a flare of hot fighting spirit. And suddenly his arm gave way and fell to the bar. He drew free and swung it limply, shaking his head in mock soberness.

"That beats me, friend. First man I ever met with a better grip than mine."

"Had you stuck it out another thirty seconds," drawled Charterhouse, "you'd got the decision."

"Let's try the left hand for a change," suggested Manners.

"Agreeable," replied Charterhouse and braced himself once more.

Their fingers locked. This time Manners only nodded and instantly hurled all the power of his shoulders into his wrist. Charterhouse felt his sinews shaking along his arm and although he kept it upright during an interval of terrific effort, he knew he would soon lose. The pressure was too great; and after a recent struggle, he surrendered; his right hand was numb and he disliked having his left in the same condition. Manners showed surprise and stepped back, chuckling more freely.

"That restores some of my damaged prestige. We'll

have to call it a draw. You've certainly got the best right."

"Your left hand," mused Charterhouse, dashing the sweat off his face, "is better than your right. Unusual."

"It favors me in most things," agreed Manners casually. "But why didn't you make a struggle for it?"

"Never spend my strength on a losing fight," drawled Charterhouse, reaching around for a free-lunch sandwich.

"To fight another day, eh?" suggested Manners and studied his opponent with an increased attention. "That's not a bad way of looking at things. Well—"

The saloon was stunned by the roar of a revolver at the very doors. A thick yell smashed over the plaza, a man cried for help dismally. Another gun spoke, splintering the saloon's upper wall and then Angels was trembling as the two factions raced for shelter, and the burst of bullets grew. Standing in front of the crowd within Studd's, Clint saw the sweeping reaction, a paling, a darkening, a contraction of faces. John Nickum started for the door, but Buck Manners pushed him aside.

"Stay put, John. I'm the only neutral in the place. You buzzards in here stay humble. This is only some private quarrel that's exciting a few other damn fools. I'll settle it—" His long frame dived through the door and Charterhouse heard a sharp, staccato order whip all around the plaza.

"Stop this nonsense! Drop those guns, you skittish fools! Can't a couple fellows stage a fight without drawing in the whole of Casabella county? Cut it out—cut it out! You, yonder by the water trough, pull down that piece. If I take a hand in this, somebody's going to drop. All hands come out of shelter."

John Nickum was planted in front of the exit, fire flashing beneath his bushy brows, cowing the saloon bunch to uneasy silence. A last shot cracked across the plaza and silence fell. Nickum spoke grimly. "Box M, get to your horses. I have given my word we will ride peacefully out of town today. But I want this county to know that if war is the desire of certain elements, war is what they shall have! Outside, Box M!"

Nickum's men pushed eagerly through the doors, leaving a handful of strangely quiet loungers behind. Nero Studd's single, flat tones struck clear through the long room. "Everybody humble. I want no guns drawn in my establishment. The man who violates that rule answers personally to me. Sit down, Flake, and finish your drink."

Charterhouse, holding half a sandwich in one hand, passed out of the place and stopped on the walk. Somebody was cursing Box M with a lurid voilence back there and was in turn cursed into meekness by Studd. The plaza was alive with milling men; gunpowder swirled down the porches and a few paces off a man rolled awkwardly into the hot sun and emitted a strangled cry. Nobody paid him the least attention as he drew his last breath and died. Nickum was bellowing at his followers; Box M swung into a semimilitary column, watchfully quiet. Buck Manners galloped past the saloon leading a riderless horse which he led to an adjacent store. A girl stepped out, laden with packages; Manners bent over to take them, smiling at her and receiving some sober reply; then she was up on her horse with one graceful move and the cavalcade moved away, leaving Angels in a haze of dust and with the taint of blood.

Standing there, soberly thoughtful, Charterhouse was conscious that an element of strength had left the town, leaving it the worse for company. The men now moving restlessly toward the dead individual were not of the same clean-cut class at all, their faces belonged to a type Charterhouse had seen too often not to recognize. A loud, bitter prophecy came down the street to him. "They got Neal, damn 'em! It was the fool's own fault for trying to wash his dirty rags on a day like this! But they got him—they fired the first shot—and it ain't going to be the last by a hell of a lot! Where's Shander, where's Studd?"

A flimsy man with weak, stooping shoulders came along toward the saloon and somebody spoke his name. "Shander—say, Shander, come over here!" But the man said, "Shut up!" and cast a black glance at Charterhouse. The next moment he was inside Studd's. Charterhouse ambled across the plaza, stopping at the water trough to wash down the last of the sandwich. Going into the grateful coolness, he went for his horse. The stall was empty and his saddle and gear missing from the pegs.

Chapter *THREE*

Clint's first reaction was to race for the back way, flash a glance into an empty corral and sweep the level land in all directions. Nothing to be seen. Galloping back to the street, he let his eyes roam along all the horses in the plaza. The stable roustabout was just limping over from the saloon, dull face twitching with excitement. He stiffened when Charterhouses's hard challenge hit him.

"Where's my horse and gear? You been fiddling with something that don't belong to you?"

The roustabout was plainly startled. He broke into a trot and passed Charterhouse to spot the vacant stall. "Oh, gosh 'lmighty! Right from under my nose! Mister, I wasn't gone more'n a minute—right after the shooting! Say, look in the street. Somebody's playing a little joke on you."

"The joke ain't on me," Charterhouse grunted, boiling angry. "You've only been gone a minute, is that it? Then my outfit is somewheres around Angels. If I've got to tear this joint apart—"

"I wonder," began the roustabout, then clicked his teeth together. He shrugged his shoulders, pointing to a sign overhead: ALL PROPERTY LEFT HERE AT OWNER'S RISK. "Too bad, mister. But there's been a powerful crowd in Angels today. I'm sorry I was away, but it wouldn't 'a' done me no good if I was here. If a fellow had wanted that horse, he could of took it and told me to butt out. I'm only working here."

"Who owns this joint?"

"Studd."

Studd and Shander were crossing the plaza at that particular moment, deep in talk. Charterhouse waited until they reached the walk and then addressed the saloonkeeper curtly. "You may not be responsible, Studd, but

26

that don't help me. Somebody's made off with around five hundred dollars of my horseflesh and gear. What do you aim to do about it?"

Studd jerked up his head in surprise. "Stole a horse from my stable? Like hell! Corbin—where was you?"

"I only left the place a minute to get me a snifter," said the roustabout sullenly. "I guess I got that right, when I work sixteen hours a day."

Studd pushed the man aside and walked in. Shander's brilliant eyes skimmed over Charterhouse. "You the fellow old Nickum talked uncivil to?"

"What of it?" retorted Charterhouse. "What's that got to do with my horse?"

"Nothing or everything," rasped Shander. He looked like a man physically ill; and in truth his skinny body was nothing but a shell. Joints showed through his loose clothing, his pigeon shoulders were too small for his head. The very brightness of his eyes seemed unhealthy. "Nothing or everything. You'll learn a lot if you stay around Casabella much."

"I'll stay till I find that horse, you just lay a bet on that," stated Charterhouse bluntly. Nero Studd came back in time to hear it, and he nodded.

"I don't blame you a bit. That horse made a pretty sight. Saw him myself."

"Well, what do you aim to do about it?" pressed Charterhouse.

Studd assumed an inscrutable air and looked at Shander. Charterhouse thought some kind of signal passed between them, though there was nothing definite about it. Then the saloonkeeper turned to inspect this tall man of the range more thoroughly.

"I can't replace your outfit. But I'll give you a good pony and good leather to sashay around and see can you find any trace of the thief. If you ain't lucky, I'll stand responsible for the difference in price. How's that?"

"Get me an outfit, I'm going to move. Won't be the first time I've trailed. I'll find my rig if I have to settle down and raise a family in Casabella."

Studd shifted to the roustabout. "Get the bay, Corbin,

and my best leather. Hustle along, the gent wants to ride. Hell of it is there won't be no tracks to do you any good, Charterhouse. Ground's all muffled up with men coming and going today. Damned if I ain't sorry."

"You save your sorrow for the fellow that did the rustling," Charterhouse advised him and turned after the roustabout. Five minutes later he was out again, riding the substitute.

Studd broke off a low-pitched conversation with Shander. "Remember, I'll stand good for the difference. And if there's any favor I can do you, let me know. Sometimes I can be right useful to folks. Bear that in mind."

Charterhouse nodded and trotted northward in the path of the Box M outfit. It was useless to seek a trail among so many scuffed prints. But up yonder in the distance was the promise of wooded country which he meant to gain. From there he might sweep the land for stray riders; and timber was itself a possible hiding place. Not daring to press his mount too hard, he settled into a steady pace. "Favors from Studd, I bet, bear a return date with compound interest. That horse of mine might be right inside Angels this minute. If so, what could I do about it? I've got to play innocent and hold my cards high."

His last guess was dead center. No sooner had he cleared the town when Studd beckoned Corbin from the stable. "Who got the gent's outfit?"

"Pawl and Stuke Rennert. Horse is in the vacant lodge hall."

Studd nodded, at which Shander asked a question. "What did you do that for?"

"Good horse," opined Studd. "And I figured it might keep this Charterhouse around Cassabella for a while. We might need him."

"I don't intend to trust anything to a stranger," countered Shander.

"No-o, but he might be a good peg to hang some blame on. Ever think of that?"

"I doubt it," said Shander. "The lines are drawn too tight. What happens from now in is going to be pretty much in the open. No use trying to fool Nickum. He

knows it's a case of simple and pure war. The bucket's
tipped over. What he don't know is the amount of help
we've got. Curly is coming to see me tonight. Curly's got
thirty first-rate hands. Nickum don't savvy that."

"What you going to do with 'em?"

"Remains to be seen," rasped Shander. "Mebbe we'll
nibble off a little chunk of Box M's stuff, mebbe we'll ar-
range to get some of his outfit out of call and tend to
them. Mebbe a straight fight, no favors asked. But the
other thing is already settled for tomorrow morning."

"Where?" asked Studd.

"Red Draw, same spot his lad was killed."

"Why pick on the same location? That ain't bright.
How you going to get him there?"

"That's fixed. We got a simple, easy way of bringing
him thataway. Just him and Haggerty." For some reason
the two men grinned maliciously.

Studd poked a black thumb under the brim of his hat.
"Didn't I say the stranger would come in handy? Nickum
burnt his nose. Everybody heard it. What's hard about
laying the blame on Mister Charterhouse?"

"What's the use of beating about the bush?" queried
Shander. "We don't need any excuse. Once Nickum's
gone, who is going to be interested in tracing down the
reason for his killing? You run too much to this secret ho-
cus-pocus."

"Stood me well in my affairs, Shander. May again. I
never leave any loose strings if I can help it. What's orders
from headquarters?"

"I'll know tonight," said Shander and swung away.
"I'm riding home."

As Charterhouse rode, the land gradually lifted him
and he began to command a more sweeping view of Casabella's vastness. The trees advanced slowly, the burning
sun packed the heat layers more thickly against the
ground, and the afternoon began to shimmer and drone.
To his left a trail split away from the main stem and shot
into the narrow mouth of a canyon that burrowed directly
into the increasing elevation. For a considerable time he

paralleled this, then lost it. But as he approached the summit of the ridge and the trees stood thinly around him, he found himself halted in a beaten area and looking down two hundred feet into sunless bottom.

Clint had often heard of Red Draw in his travels, for it was one of those natural freaks of nature worthy of more than a passing glance. Today he gave it only that and pressed on to thicker timber, finding the heat more oppressive in the shade than elsewhere. Eventually he came to a sort of knob that allowed him a full vista eastward.

Mile after mile the land stretched away, dimming with haze, empty of life, infinitely barren. Just visible was the low, bluish outline of a sprawling set of hills which, much riding experience told him, would be also barren and shelterless. Yet it was the kind of country Clint Charterhouse loved; here was room for a man to turn around, here was solitude; in short, this was cattle land, sweeping free and trackless. On impulse he left the trail that beckoned him deeper into timber and cut down into the open. To his left about a half mile, the piece of a house was visible, but he gave it no attention.

The suppressed, burning anger that had carried him out of town was now subsiding. Always the open trail had the power to soothe him like this, to whisper that another day would come and another chance present itself. The immense freedom of the prairie by day, the vaulted mystery by night—the appeal of it was in his blood and would be forever.

Three months ago he had been a responsible ranch foreman in the still farther west. Seasons of hard work behind, more seasons of hard work ahead. Sitting in the shade of a corral, he had thought about the back trail and in that instant the discovery every man makes sooner or later flashed devastatingly before him. He was twenty-six and the fine, fresh years of youth were going swiftly by. At the thought of it the savor of his cigarette went flat and all the old familiar objects about him became unsatisfactory. In the very heyday of physical and mental vigor what had he to look back upon but solemn plodding, and what could he look forward to but a straight and uneventful trail that in time dipped over the last hill? He had smoked the cigarette down to the end, risen and resigned to an astonished boss. Twenty minutes later he was riding forth, footloose and fancy free, neither knowing what he was to do or where he was to go. But he did know that the vast loneliness of the prairie impelled him to ride out and have a last taste of the heady, reckless days.

"What's life for?" he murmured now to the brassy sky. "A little work, a little to eat, a little to drink—and then a sleep. It ain't enough. Every man's got the right to look back on some piece of foolishness. Well, if I stay around Casabella, I'll get all the foolishness I can absorb. Storm brewing, clouds in the distance. It'll be a bloody welter when it gets going and nothing in God's green earth can stop it. If I was wise, I'd keep right on going. But I'm tired of being wise—and I'm looking for a horse." Range wars were always grim affairs, but while his mind condemned the impulse to stay, his blood pulsed with a tightening excitement.

He thought of Buck Manners, trying to match the inconsistencies of the man's nature. "Easy-going, packed full of deviltry, strong as a horse, laughs at most everything. But that grin conceals a heap of energy. I'd hate to be on the wrong side of any quarrel he was in. A left-handed, yellow-haired hellion. Nickum—he's true stuff, but why did he have to give me the razmataz?"

Something brought him out of his long study. At the last glance he had been surrounded by emptiness. Now, out of the northeast, grew a fan-shaped cloud with a black core, a little like the image of a baby cyclone snorting across the prairie. In time the black core became a solid, moving shape and that in turn shifted to individual riders abreast. They were aiming at him; he knew that because their angle of travel was always broadside to him as he jogged sedately along. He swept the country on all other sides and narrowed his hazel eyes. "Seem to think they have business with me. Wonder if this is to be a formal or informal party?" He shifted in the saddle, let his finger tips brush the butt of his gun, and pulled down the rim of his hat. His shadow grew longer and the burning rays of a sinking sun began to catch the back of his head. The party had swerved to cut in front of him. Never varying the even tempo of his march, he was presently confronted by ten Box M riders, Driver Haggerty and Heck Seastrom to the fore. He halted. Haggerty's stringy, unpleasant wedge of a face poked forward.

"What you doing here?"

"What of it?" countered Charterhouse.

"You know the rules," stated Haggerty, grinding down on his chew.

Clint stared at the group emotionlessly. "I'm acquainted with the general rules of the road, yeah. But I can't nowise keep up with a lot of tinhorn house rules that some of these rinkydink counties keep making and changing. What rules do you happen to allude to?"

"The deadline's what I mean," grunted Haggerty, increasingly sullen. "How come you're over it?"

"Don't recall any chalk marks or fences or deep sea buoys on the road. What deadline?"

"This ain't a fence country, brother. If you come from one, better get the hell back there. You're on Box M land, three miles deep from the deadline. What's your business?"

"My business is minding my business," allowed Charterhouse calmly. I seem to have trouble doing it. You Box M buzzards sure seem awful proud of a few sand-blistered sections that ain't worth spitting on. How do you get that way? What misled you into believing the Lord personally anointed this scope of range anyhow?"

"I wouldn't get salty," growled Haggerty, a higher gleam of temper in his red eyes. "You may be a sure-enough stranger and again mebbe you ain't. Pretty sassy, seems to me. Talked real large to old John, didn't you? How would you like to be left afoot out here and cool off?"

"That's just the kind of an Indian I got you pegged to be."

"Yeah?" snarled Haggerty. "Well, I'm apt to show you some more tricks besides. You know what happens to a man on the wrong side of the deadline?"

Charterhouse studied the group. Excepting for Seastrom they sat like so many sacks of meal, slant-eyed and hostile, just exactly the kind of men to take their instructions seriously. Seastrom grinned frankly at him and built a cigarette with a slightly bored air.

"Listen," said Charterhouse, using diplomacy's siren tongue, "I am aiming to ride across this flea-bit stretch of country and pass out of it. You boys have maybe swallowed enough of this real estate to consider you have a vested interest in it, which is all right with me. When I reach this said deadline I'll brush off my clothes so's I won't be packing any of your sacred soil away. That fair?"

"You'll do just what I say you'll do," grunted Haggerty.

Seastrom chuckled. "Hell's fire, Haggerty, he's all right. How could he know about a deadline? Let him fog on."

"Shut up. I'll attend to this business."

"Yeah?" murmured Seastrom, very mild. "You make another break like that to me and I'll begin to proceed to commence. I'm not your official pants buttoner."

The two men swapped long glances. Haggerty's sour face flushed up a little and he jerked his elbow at Charterhouse. "Get out of here. Ride three miles south—and stay out! You've had your warning and next time you're caught there won't be any debate."

"Check," agreed Charterhouse, gathering his reins. "Being slapped twice today by your virtuous outfit, I'm beginning to feel you don't really admire me. Life's pretty short, Haggerty, to be so serious-minded. If I meet you again on open territory, I might enlarge on the subject."

Haggerty jammed his horse against Charterhouse. "If you want to make any speeches to me, go ahead."

"Never play another man's game," observed Charterhouse.

"I thought so! Beat it, yellow-belly!"

"I'll bear that in mind," said Charterhouse without a trace of inflection. Swinging, he rode off, hearing Seastrom's lazy comment.

"You're a fool, Haggerty. Crooked or straight, that man ain't meek enough to swallow those remarks. You stepped over the line." Then the party gathered up and swept westward.

Charterhouse maintained the same level pace and the same indolent posture. But he was afire again, the hazel eyes stormy. The long nose pinched in at the nostrils and his mouth made a long thin line across the bronzed skin. The horse, without pressure, began to quicken and grew restless.

"Easy," said Charterhouse softly. "Plenty of time, plenty of time. Long day and another one coming. I see I have got more business than looking for stolen gear. Evidently Mister Haggerty has forgotten men are supposed to stand accountable for their remarks. That's a lesson he will be soon taught."

Since he had given his word to cross some imaginary deadline, he kept it stolidly—bearing constantly to the south. The sun sank and blue twilight began to fill up the arroyos like running water. Off easterly was the spread of a ranch and he curved for it while the moon strengthened in the sky and night fell down soundlessly and mysteriously. Then the lull of twilight was gone and a coyote mournfully announced the parade of night creatures. A yellow beam winked across the prairie, cutting through a velvet blackness that seemed to absorb the pale effort of the moon. The pony breathed beneath him, bridle chains tinkled—and elsewhere were only the musical reverberations of the earth.

Ears tuned to this, Clint was suddenly aware of a deep, subdued drumming ahead. Horsemen curved out of yonder space and cut across the beam of light one at a time. Perhaps three, perhaps ten. He couldn't tell. But they had drawn into the ranch. When he arrived in front of the main house, he saw the shadowed horses waiting and heard talk coming out of the open front door. He eased himself, thought it over a long moment and hailed the place. The talk cut off. A man blocked the area of light coming through the portal and then swiftly moved away from it, standing on the porch.

"Light and come in," was the curt welcome.

Charterhouse sidled his pony to the end of the porch and stepped off. "Passing through," was all he said, considering he had stated his needs sufficiently for any man versed in range hospitality. But the host's reply seemed long in coming and reserved in manner. "Step in," was all he said.

Charterhouse walked through the door, expecting to confront others. But the room was empty. A whisky bottle and several glasses were on a table, some half filled; tobacco smoke still curled in the light. Swinging about, he saw Shander follow through and stop, queerly watchful. "So—the stranger?" he muttered.

"Sure seems like I keep butting into the same list of people around here," rejoined Charterhouse gravely.

"Population of Casabella ain't so large," said Shander rather dryly. "And most of us shift ground in a hurry. You are welcome to my place. I'll have one of the boys put up your horse."

Warning struck Charterhouse like the clang of a fire bell. "If you don't mind," he answered, "I'll partake of a bite and pass on. Night riding's easy on the horse."

Shander's lips twitched sardonically. "Reckon that would depend what sort of night riding it was, wouldn't it?" A new idea diverted his line of thought. "I came out of Angels right behind you. Funny I didn't draw abreast along the way."

"Me, I cut for the timber country and then swung east."

"That would be in Box M territory," suggested Shander, eyes riveted on his guest. Charterhouse saw suspicion coiled in the man's eyes.

"Yeah," he agreed. "I found out about that later."

"How so?" asked Shander, driving the question home.

"Committee came out and spent a few minutes of their good time instructing me as to Casabella's lines and corner posts." Charterhouse rolled a cigarette, grinning slightly as if the memory amused him. But his nerves kept tightening up as he stood there facing that gaunt rancher with the sick body and burning glance. And though the house was quite still, he felt the presence of a great many other men just beyond sight, listening in on his words. Shander cleared his throat.

"I'll not bother you with rules," said he with plain courtesy. "Come along and I'll see you get a snack." He led the way through a back door into a dining room and lifted his voice. "Vasco—boil the coffee." And he bowed his head slightly at Charterhouse. "Excuse the lack of company. I've got a little business to take care of."

He went out as a Mexican came in from the kitchen and laid a platter of boiled beef and potatoes in front of Charterhouse. The latter fell to, not yet rid of the feeling he was under observation. Judging from the stacked dishes the men of the outfit had already eaten. Savoring his meal with the gusto of a hungry traveler, he heard footsteps tramping through the front room. Somebody swore and a general murmur of conversation eddied meaninglessly back to him. Vasco returned from the kitchen with a tin of pie and the coffee pot, leaving both for Charterhouse's pleasure. Dallying with his food, Charterhouse posted up his silent observations.

"Den of forty thieves. Couldn't of horned into a worse joint. Everything I do today is wrong and getting wronger. I don't feel right and I don't feel very damned safe. Sooner I ride off the better it's going to be. But I ain't so sure—"

He rolled a cigarette and rose to go into the front room. He knew he would face additional men but he was not prepared for the crowd that fronted him when he pushed open the door. Fifteen or twenty of them, with here and there an individual he thought he had previously seen in Angels. But familiar or strange, they were a woolly, bitten lot, a stolid and unpleasant set of characters. Nor was it reassuring to realize that they had come out of hiding; either they felt he was harmless or could soon be rendered harmless. Shander lolled in a chair and waved at the center table.

"Help yourself to the bottle. Welcome to the party."

Charterhouse grinned. "Should of brought my invite. Must have left it home on the bureau top."

"Doubt if it makes any difference," said Shander, hard

amusement cropping out. "Main point is you're here and among friends."

"I was wondering about that last point," mused Charterhouse, helping himself from a bottle.

"You're not deaf or dumb," said Shander, "and you seem able to add round numbers. So you can make up your own mind about the friend business. Said you come through the timber and circled east at the Bowlus place?"

"I came through the timber," replied Charterhouse. "I don't make this Bowlus place you mention. But there was a house off a ways."

"See anybody there?"

Charterhouse liked the tang of his liquor and decided for another, all the while feeling the increased pressure of attention from these taut-cheeked men. He was going through the grist mill, no doubt of that.

"No-o, it looked like empty country to me."

"How many in the Box M party that stopped you?"

Charterhouse considered. "Six, eight—ten, I gather."

"Any familiar faces?"

"Seastrom . . . Haggerty."

This seemed to contain meat. There was a slight shifting, a covert passage of glances. Through the smoke he made out a white-faced youngster sitting in a dark corner and staring at him like an unwinking reptile. Shander pressed on.

"Which way did they go after they left you?"

"Struck westward," stated Charterhouse and put down his glass very carefully. "And with that answered, school's out for old man Charterhouse's little boy."

Shander's mouth tipped down at the corners. "Considered you've paid for your supper, uh?"

"In my country," Charterhouse drawled, "a guest owns the house as long as he is in it, no questions asked, no pay taken."

"Nice sentiment—for a peaceful land," admitted Shander and seemed to be unpleasantly affected by the remark. He rolled his cigar between fingers. "But we have to do different in Casabella."

"I am making a stab at playing neutral, Shander. What I see or hear I keep to myself."

"Also impossible in Casabella."

"I have bought no chips in this game," Charterhouse remarked.

"Beg to differ. You have."

"As how?"

"By stepping into Angels, for one thing. By having your nose blistered at Nickum's hands for another. By having your horse stole. By being chased across the deadline. If I'm any judge of human nature, you can't truthfully say it is your intention to ride out of Casabella and call it quits."

"It was a point I was debating," admitted Charterhouse.

"I was betting you'd already made up your mind," countered Shander, seeming to enjoy himself. Light gleamed against his eyes. "Sit down and take life easy."

"I'd prefer to ride," said Charterhouse with a great deal more casualness than he felt.

"Couldn't think of turning a guest out this late. It wouldn't be seemly. I've had one of the boys put up your horse."

"In other words, I do what I'm told," challenged Charterhouse.

"Good guess. You're old enough to know why?"

"I have been known to do some private thinking," agreed Charterhouse. "Well, I never argue with a better run of cards than mine. And if this whisky holds out, what difference does it make?"

Shander's sick face broke into lines of cynical humor, and he was on the point of speaking again when the youngster in the dark corner rose and pushed himself toward the table with a swagger of shoulders. In full light Charterhouse saw a triangular face, strangely pallid and as smooth as a woman's, with a pair of eyes as pale and unwavering as he had ever marked. A lock of silky hair escaped the brim of a floppy hat and fell down in front of each ear. A kid with a dirty face stood there, smiling a little, yet without the slightest humor; a vain, boasting youngster armed to the teeth. He squared himself at Charterhouse.

"Ever see me before?"

"Haven't had the pleasure."

"I'm Curly. You know who I am now?"

"Your reputation is known to me," admitted Charterhouse truthfully. There was no man in the state more notorious than this youthful bandit.

"What's this for?" complained Shander.

"So he'll know me when he sees me again," grinned Curly and turned away. "Seems like we've done a smear of talking and got nowhere."

Shander nodded. "Chaterhouse, I expect you're pretty tired. We'll excuse you. Louey, escort the guest to the bunkhouse, and stay there yourself."

"I had just got to drinking good," mourned Charterhouse and walked through the crowd. "Thanks for the hospitality, Shander, and I hope you have pancakes for breakfast. My favorite dish."

His guard ambled out behind him; they crossed the porch and stepped down to the soft earth. Horses nodded patiently in the darkness and one groaned dismally right beside Charterhouse. He had the stub of a dead cigarette in his mouth and halted to find a match, while Louey, not particularly interested, stood a yard off and waited.

"Damn," grunted Charterhouse, breaking his first match. He searched himself once more, eyes questing through the shadows. "Pass me a light, will you?"

As he said it, he began marching forward again, toward the dim shadow of the bunkhouse. Louey fell in step, both hands dropping into his pockets. Charterhouse veered slightly, gun ripping out of its seat, rising and smashing across the solid head of Shander's man. He fell and lay sprawling. Charterhouse whirled and checked an almost irresistible impulse to run for the horses; instead he walked quietly up to the nearest animal, reached for the trailing ribbons and stepped into the saddle. From the angle of the yard he was able to look through the open door of the house and see part of the crowd as they shifted about the room, with Shander risen and tramping around the table. He even caught a stray word or two. "... to-morrow, but otherwise ..." Pulling the horse clear of the porch, he suddenly stiffened, all nerves like cold drawn wire. Somebody walked out of the desert, saw him, and casually hailed.

"Who's that—where you going?"

"Back in a minute," muttered Charterhouse.

"What for?" demanded the other. Talk in the house stopped; boots tramped over the boards as Charterhouse increased the distance intervening. The man swore glumly. "Quit sucking your tongue and talk up. Who is it?"

Then Shander's voice echoed flatly. "Who is that? Hold on—draw in! Louey, where are you? Louey! where are you? Louey! Stop that horse or—"

Charterhouse sank his spurs and the pony lurched into a swift burst of speed. The night was split apart by a shot, then a second, both whipping wide; Shander yelled and his crew came beating out to the porch. More explosions blasted the shadows. Charterhouse, drawing into the pro-tecting darkness, heard a vast volume of swearing as that unruly crew fought their pitching horses. He had this much grace, this margin of safety and he rowled the sturdy beast beneath him unmercifully. Yet, pointed due eastward, he caught the peaked outline of Shander's barn right beside him and there flashed across his mind another expedient. If he kept going straight, they would pick up the drum of his flight or catch his silhouette against the horizon; if he swung now— Obeying the impulse, Clint shot for the barn, rode against a side wall and stopped dead. The deep gloom folded about him. A few riders sped by easterly and then the bulk of the party pounded past. Somebody yelled an order to spread out fanwise. Another rider veered near and skirted Charterhouse no more than ten feet away. Then the thud and jangle of their progress dimmed, leaving him safe for the moment.

But as he gathered the reins and decided to ease gradu-ally away in a southerly direction, he discovered himself trapped. Voices advanced from the house and a tardy horseman came around from the other end of the barn and jogged circularly about the ranch, apparently on guard against surprise. The voices came nearer. Two men talking. One was Shander, whose irritable tones began to carry distinct meaning.

"I never trust anybody. He may be one of Nickum's damned spies, for all we know. That palaver in the saloon between the two could easily have been faked. You got to remember old John knows all the tricks of the trade. We're not up against a greenhorn."

"Sure. But this Charterhouse probably was telling a straight yarn." That, Charterhouse decided, was Curly. "I take it so. He just got scared and figured to pass out. I give him credit for guts, the way he pounded Louey down. I could use fellas like that."

"I don't trust anybody," repeated Shander, seeming to be nearer. "But he didn't hear anything important, if he was Nickum's man. Nickum already knows you and me are hooked up. All our cards have been exposed except one, which is how many men you've got collected. I want that held secret. You see to it nobody rides away from you. Keep a strict hand on your gang."

"Well, what's the next play? I got thirty-five tough nuts, and I can't keep 'em entertained by playing duck on a rock all day in Dead Man. Those fellows want to see action. Elsewise they'll pull freight."

"Everything depends on what happens in the morning," countered Shander. "Once Nickum is knocked over, the gate's wide open to us."

"Where's it going to happen?"

"Same place his kid was killed. On the trail to Angels, beside Red Draw where the trees thin down. Remember those three rocks in a row? That's the spot. Him and Haggerty will be coming alone. About ten in the morning, figuring them to start from Box M Ranch at eight, which is Nickum's habit."

"How'd you engineer this business, anyhow? What makes you so sure he'll be riding along there?"

"That's all taken care of by the other party. Let's go back to the house."

Charterhouse waited until their talk dwindled away. Then, knowing that any longer delay would narrow his chance of safe flight, he pushed the pony along the barn wall until he came to the corner. The mournful whistling of the riding guard approached. Some of the pursuers were straggling back. Charterhouse quelled a strong impulse to break and run, silently cursing this laggard riding guard who slid in front of him and slowly curved to the north. A shout came out of the distance, answered by another. Charterhouse slipped on into the open, scanning every inch of the shadows between barn and house. The Mexican cook walked out of a back door and dumped a pan of water. The sound evoked a clear call from a returning man.

"Say, he musta ducked into a hole around here! It ain't scarcely reasonable he coulda fell off the edge of the earth so sudden. How about looking around the yard? Anybody done it?"

Charterhouse was three hundred feet away and increasing the distance at a pace that seemed slower than crawling. He began to sweat, expecting at any moment to have them catch sight of his fugitive silhouette and come charging down. They were alive and excitable back there, like a pack of hounds trying to catch the scent of a rabbit. Lanterns bobbed; a strong party circled the barn rapidly; he felt rather than saw a second party driving straight at him. His horse walked down the lip of an arroyo and hesitated. Charterhouse drew a long breath, swung with the arroyo and increased speed. Presently he pulled out of the arroyo and cut a circle in the desert and never stopped until Shander's place was a mile southward, light still winking through the fog.

"Time to pause and consider," he mused. "I'm in a bad hole. One side or the other, it's open season on me. If I had the sense of a cooked flea, I'd turn and put the boundaries of this doggoned county away behind. So they are going to kick old John Nickum down the chute? Well, what of it? I don't owe him any favors. If he considers he don't need anybody's help, then I sure haven't got a call to butt in. No sir, I ought to turn."

Common sense told him to retreat. Therefore he did exactly the opposite thing, squared himself by the high, dim stars and settled into a steady jog eastward. Soon after he had crossed the deadline again, bound for the timbered ridge.

"Less than twelve hours from now—and hell to pay prob'ly. Well, I'm getting my wish."

Chapter FOUR

From his hide-out in the trees a few hours later, Clint Charterhouse looked down into a small meadow sparkling with dew the early morning's sun had not yet dissipated. A cabin, a barn and a corral stood here. Wisps of smoke rose from the cabin and a cow browsed at the end of a picket, bell clinking melodiously in the still, fresh air. Out of the barn stalked a cattle dog whose baying had been in Charterhouse's ears all during the night; and the dog crossed to the cabin to sit on its haunches and stare directly upward at the trees. The door opened. A wizened and shabby old man stepped out with a tin pail. For a moment he lifted his head to the sky and nodded at the fine, crisp air as if he found it good; then he went over to the cow and knelt down to milk. It seemed to Charterhouse that the fellow walked awkwardly, with a great deal of hesitation, and his impression was confirmed a little later when, milking done, the man rose and came back, stumbling over some small tuft of earth.

"Kind of feeble," guessed Charterhouse. "And none too safe, if he's alone. Must be the one they called Bowlus."

The man stopped at the doorway and swung about to face the hillside. His high-pitched voice took Charterhouse by complete surprise. "If you're hungry, come on down to breakfast."

"Hell, what's given me away?" muttered Charterhouse. He thought a moment, sharply studying the clearing. The old fellow spoke again.

"Don't worry none. It ain't the first time I've had visitors on the dodge. Come on down."

Charterhouse chuckled and stood up. He brought his horse to the edge of the trees and went down alone. A closer inspection of the man erased his humor. The poor

devil was blind, or nearly so; that explained the stumbling, and also the guide ropes that lay on the ground and
extended out from the cabin to the barn and to the corral.

"Can't see as good as I used to," explained the man,
feeling Charterhouse's inspection. "My dog does that for
me. He's been a-fretting most of the night, and so I
knowed you was making a dry camp yonder. I'm Bowlus
and there ain't a drop of unfriendliness in me for man or
beast. What I know, I keeps to m'self. I can't see you and
I don't know what you look like. So I wouldn't be no help
to a posse at all, would I? And I'm too old to be shot for
harboring folks like you. So we're both safe. Come in."

The room was as tidy as any proud housewife's kitchen.
Bacon and coffee smell wafted up from the stove, a bunk
was neatly made and a row of utensils hung in orderly
row against the wall. Charterhouse chuckled when he
glanced at the table; it was set for two.

"Pretty shrewd. I can see you know your country pretty
well."

"Sit down. Pitch into the larrup and bread. You most
likely are in a haste. Gen'ly speaking you boys are. Well,
I've had all kinds of 'em, and they've treated me fair.
Law enforcing ain't my business and I don't purpose to
stand at my door with a gun. Can't help it if this cabin's
right on the trail between coming and going. Yessir, I've
seen lots of 'em. Some undeniably bad, mister; some as
good as the best. Never can tell about a man. I've had
'em pressed so hard they wouldn't no more'n get beyond
the barn afore the sheriff or a posse was swamping down
from the trail. Here's the bacon and coffee. Pitch right in."

"I'm not in such a hurry," explained Charterhouse and
waited until the man had settled across from him. "But I
ain't anxious to be seen in the wrong places."

"So it's come to that already?" muttered old Bowlus. "I
knowed it would, ever since Nickum's boy was killed up
by the Draw. Another bloody hell. Casabella politics. I
dunno who you are or where you come from, but unless
somebody's hired your gun you'd be better off by departing in peace. Say, you ain't that Charterhouse stranger
which had his horse stole?"

"How do you know?" grunted Charterhouse, surprised again.

"I keep abreast o' things pretty well," said Bowlus shrewdly. "Fought in one of these wars twenty years ago, with Nickum. You bet I'm a Nickum man, skin and hair. Ev'rybody knows it, but I'm too old to draw any trouble from the other side."

"You might be talking to a man from the other side right now," suggested Charterhouse.

Bowlus rose and carried his cup to the stove for another jot of coffee which he drank standing up. "No-o," he decided, "you ain't got that kind of a voice."

"I'm obliged for the meal," said Charterhouse and quietly slipped a silver dollar on the table. Bowlus wasn't even looking in that direction but he spoke quickly.

"I didn't ask you for that, mister."

"You haven't got anything wrong with your sight," grinned Charterhouse. "Never mind, you can't furnish a free lunch to promiscuous travelers. I appreciate the—"

A silvery-sounding hail floated across the meadow. Charterhouse squared for the door but Bowlus was already there.

"Never mind. It's Sherry Nickum. She comes to buy milk off me. I got the only producing cow in Casabella."

Charterhouse heard her draw in and slip to the ground, speaking with a kind of gay gustiness to the old man. "A little early this morning, Henry. Had to duck away. There's trouble coming and they don't want me to ride alone any more. I've got a couple of dressed hens here for you. I—"

She was framed in the doorway, startled to silence by the sight of Charterhouse; a tall, lazy-eyed girl with a mass of copper red hair rebelliously trying to escape a scarlet turban. She was in riding breeches and boots and her sturdy shoulders unconsciously straightened before him; a flare of interest came to her slim face. The rounding lips seemed about to quirk into a smile and then pursed together as if forbidding it. Charterhouse took off his hat and nothing on earth could have forbidden his frank, glimmering humor.

"Henry," he drawled, "you're a lucky man, even without the gift of those hens."

She considered this with perfect gravity. He felt himself being weighed and tallied by the long, level glance that ended with a sedate murmur to Bowlus. "I see you're running your restaurant for strayed pilgrims again."

Charterhouse chuckled. "Shot plumb through the heart by an off-hand bullet."

She walked to the table and placed a basket on it, by chance touching the dollar Charterhouse had laid there. That brought her eyes quickly back to him with an expression slightly puzzled and more friendly. Bowlus, still at the door, tranquilly made explanation.

"This is the fellow that had his horse stole in Angels, Sherry."

"The name," said Clint, "is Charterhouse."

She sat on the edge of the bunk and tapped the floor with one boot heel. "So you're that man? Do you know you are being talked about? My dad doubts you, Seastrom thinks you are about *it*, good or bad, and Buck Manners respects you for doing what nobody else ever did to him before."

"Accident," mused Charterhouse, marking the melody of her voice.

"Hardly that. Nobody wins from Buck by accident. They earn their victories."

"Reckon you know him better than I do," agreed Charterhouse. "Right now I'm most interested in finding out what your own opinion is."

He found she had a grave manner of considering his words in lengthening silence. A flicker of impish delight appeared in the gray eyes, followed by a deliberate answer.

"I ought to know about Buck, being engaged to him."

He failed to put on his poker face quickly enough. She saw his features settle and cloud. For some reason she dropped her eyes, flushing.

"My apologies," said he gently, "for asking fool questions."

"I didn't consider it foolish," said she, and drew all the

sting out of his new knowledge with a warming smile. "I hear you are looking for work. Buck Manners could use good hands any time."

"I've sort of been discouraged."

"Don't let anything my father says bother you. He ... he has had many worries."

"Where's he now, home?" broke in Bowlus.

"Started to Angels on business after I pulled out," said the girl.

Charterhouse looked at his watch. "Time for me to be on my way. I'm inside the Box M deadline, which Mister Haggerty doesn't like."

"Haggerty's a fool sometimes," retorted the girl energetically. "He doesn't use his head and his tongue's too bitter."

"I observe," said Charterhouse. He turned to Bowlus. "No objections to my bringing down the pony for a drink?"

"Help yourself."

The girl had risen, still looking at Charterhouse. "If you are bound out of this country, good luck." There was a small wistfulness about the words that drew him around and roused some latent recklessness.

"Supposing I'm staying around here for a while—what then?"

Her answer was long in coming. "Still—good luck," said she and met his eyes squarely.

He bowed and went out, climbing the slope for his horse and returning to the well by the cabin. She was in the doorway and as he lifted a full bucket and turned the pony to it, he heard her speak with a sudden change of tone. He looked up to find cold suspicion on her face. "You've got a horse with Shander's brand on it!"

"Yeah," he drawled. "I had to borrow it under pressing circumstances. I—"

"Then I can wish you no luck at all," cried Sherry Nickum angrily. "I hate Shander. I hate any man who works for Shander, accepts Shander's help, or even speaks to Shander! I wish you no luck—and get off Nickum range!"

The pony drank to the bottom of the bucket. Charterhouse, never moving a muscle of his countenance, swung to the saddle and pulled about to face the girl's straight and rigid figure in the doorway. He caught something of old John Nickum's unbending, fighting spirit in her at that moment; a flash of the same imperious temper. And though the picture she made brought back his own vision of all that was fine and desirable in a woman, he was stung badly by the scornful fire of her eyes and the sudden bitter distrust. Nor did it help him to know that she belonged rightfully to another man, a man of power and influence far above his own. So he bowed with stiff courtesy and gathered the pony.

"When wishes change so soon, Sherry Nickum, it is better not to have them at all. Since you do not mean to be friendly, I will forget your first friendly words." He rode into the timber, never looking back.

The farther Clint traveled the more the injury smarted. "Slapped again," he muttered. "Seems to me I'm taking an undue amount of punishment. What's the matter with the looks of my face? Or has everybody gone crazy of a sudden?" His own clear sight told him that the threat of range war was responsible for all this touchiness and hard suspicion. But even so, it was a distinct blow to his pride to know that others failed to see the prevailing honesty of his impulses. Was the dividing line in Casabella so thin that people refused to trust all outward appearances? "Saint Peter," he grumbled, "would get run out of Casabella for being suspected of sheepherding. I never saw such a state of affairs."

For quite a long length of time Clint Charterhouse forgot the nature of his business. Not until he arrived at the top of the ridge and came upon a small glade flooded with the golden morning's light did he think much about his reasons for returning this way. The main trail leading north and south kept to the high ground; that trail he had followed out of Angels the day before. Upon it were many hoofprints but none fresh enough to have been made that morning. Old John Nickum had not yet passed down, if indeed the cattleman meant to come this way at all. Considering the problem, Charterhouse wondered why Shander was so very sure Nickum would keep to the trail. There was something queer about that, something that did not meet the eye. Yet he had no time at present to dig into the mystery; Nickum was on the way and possibly would soon pass by. Another half mile would bring the bluff old baron to the edge of timber and up against the rim of Red Draw. At some place along that draw the trap was set. Shander had said so and there was no doubting the man's grim, ruthless sincerity on that point.

"What of it?" Charterhouse asked himself. "Slapped three times and here I stand asking for more. A bigger damn fool never came out of the shell. Nobody's asked me to butt into this business. So why don't I roll my hoop?"

The drumming of a woodpecker shot through the trees with a startling clarity, rousing him from all this tedious thinking. No matter how little license he had for intruding on the quarrel, he had, nevertheless, lived too long with his own code to throw it over now. His reason told him that Nickum and Nickum's adherents were in the right; Shander was certainly on the opposite side of the fence— and he had always hated the kind of outlawry Shander stood for.

There was his answer. He would dip an oar in this muddy water and later tell Nickum to go plumb straight to hell, just for the pleasure of it. With that in mind he passed across the trail and threaded through the thickening pines. Underbrush impeded him in places and every few minutes he stopped to put an ear against the still air; presently he saw a break in the pines and he went forward on foot, to step to the very brink of Red Draw.

At this point the trees grew up to the margin and the winding of the chasm shut off his view to the south. Retreating, he led the horse parallel to the draw for a quarter mile and again crawled back to scan the freakish slash in the earth. This time he commanded a tolerably good view and made out where the pines dwindled to open country. It was open country also across the draw, but gigantic bald-faced boulders made a sort of parapet along the rim of the farther side and shut off most of his view. Still dissatisfied, he repeated the trick of retreating and paralleling until streaks of stronger light ahead told him he was very nearly arrived at the end of shelter; the trail, moreover, was sweeping nearer him. He veered farther away from it, left his pony in the deepest thicket he could find and squatted at the brink of the canyon with tightening anticipation. Shander had mentioned the spot of ambush to be near three particular rocks; and unless his eyes betrayed him, three such rocks, standing shoulder to shoulder, commanded the far side of the draw at the exact spot where the trail shot out of the trees. Thus any man coming down from the pines would present first a head-on target for anyone behind the opposite rocks; and later an exposed flank passing by. The distance across the chasm could not be much more than twenty-five feet, which made good revolver range and deadly for a rifle bullet. Yet the ambusher would be absolutely safe, for neither horse nor man could make the leap across and the bulwark of rising rocks formed perfect concealment.

"I believe this is the spot," Charterhouse mused. "But how am I going to find out? And I think I hear—"

His ears picked up some stray sound from up the trail about the same time his eyes lifted to the pine tops. Those ladder-like branches invited him up to have his look-see, which he promptly accepted. With both feet off the ground, it occurred to him that the warlike Shander partisan whose horse he had so unceremoniously borrowed, had been carrying a rifle in a saddle boot; so, chuckling to himself, and restored to much better humor at the prospect of a little excitement, he dropped out of the tree and went over to get the gun.

"This gun being used in wrong hands reminds me of a gent being caught in his own bear trap."

Faint rumors of men talking came down the ridge. Charterhouse threw open the rifle's breech, verified the waiting shell, and closed it carefully to prevent the metallic sound from telegraphing through the still air. Carrying it back to the tree, he took the first branches with consid-

erable exertion; at twenty feet he found a small break in
the greenery that gave him a partial glance across the canyon; he thought he saw the tip of some dark figure in the
stony crevices, but was not sure. The next ten feet he
climbed with cat-like caution. Right above him was a full
tunnel through the branches; and he poked his head around
the tree like some wary chipmunk. At the far end of this
sharply angled vista, sprawled full length behind an enormous stone, was a man whose shoulders were wedged into
an aperture that gave him command of the trail on this
side. He looked like a Mexican, but Charterhouse couldn't
be sure. A hundred yards rearward in a hollow stood a
waiting horse. Voices came along the trees distinctly;
whereat Charterhouse turned to catch sight of Nickum's
party and only saw a momentary passage of three riders.
"One more'n Shander figured," he reflected. Lifting his rifle, he rested it on a branch and drew full bead on the
ambusher.

In the narrowing interval of time he debated giving the
fellow a warning. He decided against it. This was war and
the man had elected to kill in the meanest way known to
the West. "Moreover," reflected Charterhouse, "if I sing
out, he's apt to rise up and take a pot shot anyhow and
run like hell, leaving me treed and openly suspected of
being some help to him. No, can't be done. Good-by,
brother."

Clint had his sights true on the man and the slack of
the trigger taken up. From the corner of his eye he saw
Nickum, Heck Seastrom and Haggerty come into the
open, single file. Haggerty's face twitched aside, staring
across the draw; after that Charterhouse saw nothing but
the hidden killer. His breath stopped; he squeezed. A
smash of sound beat over tree and rock and the clear air
rang with the splitting fragments of the echo. The ambusher jumped once, and never moved again. Haggerty
had thrown himself out of the saddle to the ground and
was firing point-blank at the rocks, emptying his gun with
a certain heedlessness. Seastrom and Nickum were still
mounted, but they had swung around and were opening
up more coolly.

"Get down!" yelled Haggerty. "He's trying to pot you! Same spot they got your son, John! Get down outa the sky!"

"Not for any Shander rat in the world!" boomed Nickum. Heck Seastrom had fired two shots with careful intent and lowered his gun.

"He's done," he called calmly. "I can see the front end of his rifle tipped down. Yeah, there's his head, flopped against the rock. We got him. Get up, Haggerty, you don't have to eat all the dirt off the trail."

Haggerty rose, squinting over the canyon. He had lost his hat, and Charterhouse had a fair chance to see the sour, sullen glare of the Box M's foreman's face as it turned from point to point. "May be more of 'em," he grunted.

"Then mebbe you had better fall on your belly again," retorted Seastrom.

"I'll take no more of that from you!" bellowed Haggerty. He squared himself at Seastrom. "Seems to me you're taking this affair some calm. Might be a reason for it."

"What would you judge?" drawled Seastrom.

"Mebbe you already knew the bullet wouldn't be for *you!*"

Seastrom reached for his papers indolently. "In other words, I knew this was a frame to get the boss, uh? To be plumb plain, I'm working for Box M but wearing Shander's britches?"

"I'll let you state the case," droned Haggerty. "You do it with a slick enough tongue."

"A-huh," Seastrom poured himself a smoke. "Brother Haggerty, you don't like me, and I don't like you. If we wasn't working for the same boss, we'd sure as fate tangle. As it is, you range louse, don't ever open your trap to me that way again or I'll just let you try that trick gun flip you've been practicing the last year. Pull in that vinegar mug and keep still."

"You boys," broke in Nickum sharply, "cut that out. I'll have no fighting in my outfit. What in hell makes you two so cagey? Quit spitting like a couple of puff adders.

You had no call to make those remarks, Haggerty. We were just foolish to walk into the same trap my son did. It won't happen again. That piece of skunk bait missed his shot—"

Charterhouse had meanwhile slipped quietly down the tree and ridden his horse to the edge of the trees. He cut into the conversation casually. "Mister Nickum, he never fired a shot. I plugged him from the top of that tree."

Haggerty whirled and let his arm half-fall toward his gun butt. Nickum boomed at his foreman and stopped the threat of gun-play, himself riding between the two. His ruddy face swept Charterhouse and then tilted to the pine tips. "You shot, uh? Let's see your gun."

Charterhouse lifted the rifle and passed it over. Nickum threw open the breech, saw the empty shell spin out, and put his nose down against the chamber. He handed it back with stiff courtesy.

"How in hell did we misjudge the sound of that bullet? It must have been pretty close. What's more important, how did you know about this business, friend?"

"Simple answer to that," drawled Charterhouse, catching Seastrom's friendly wink. "After your efficient foreman told me to get off Box M range I ran into a house yonder for the night. Shander's house. Overheard a few things and made my departure, having to borrow one of his horses sort of sudden. So I thought I'd come back to see how the play ran out."

"I'd be an ungrateful pup if I failed to make my due thanks to you," stated Nickum gruffly. "Why didn't you stop us up in the timber instead of doing it this way?"

"You think you would have believed my yarn?" challenged Charterhouse. "Not in a pig's eyes. You'd of burnt my nose again, and I'm getting kind of sensitive on the smeller."

Nickum's florid cheeks took on a deeper flush, yet the unerring instinct for justice made him admit Charterhouse's reasoning. "I reckon you have plenty of right to believe us uncharitable in judgment. Though you have got to admit nobody can afford to be overfriendly at a time like this. I will ask you to accept my apologies."

"Took, and we will consider the thing squared all around," said Charterhouse, a little embarrassed. He had nourished a healthy dislike of Nickum but now found he could not support it against such bluff fairness. Seastrom was on his stomach at the edge of the draw, peering at the rocks on the far side. Haggerty stood a few yards removed, small eyes never leaving Charterhouse, catching every move of muscle and every change of features. He seemed like a man poised for either attack or flight.

"That's a Mexican yonder," called Seastrom.

"Shander's got plenty of 'em to waste," was Nickum's blunt retort. "I don't exactly get this, Charterhouse. Since you considered yourself injured by Box M, what made you lend a hand like this?"

"I guess that's the kind of a damn fool I am," grunted Charterhouse. "Never did like to see a crook rig up a killing against a straight man. Sort of goes against the grain. But you've got a right to complain at my horning in without an invite."

"Complain, hell," said Nickum. "I'm here to offer apologies for what happened at Studd's. I'd admire to see you on my ranch. How about it?"

"Hold on, boss," intervened Haggerty. "This might be one of Shander's stunts. I'd be mighty careful about hiring the gent."

"I'll take the chance and I'll do the worrying for Box M," stated Nickum impatiently.

"If I'm foreman of your outfit, my word ought to count some," insisted Haggerty with a sullen twitch of his mouth. "Dammit, I don't like this man and I don't want to work with him."

Nickum's frosty glance remained an uncomfortably long time on Haggerty. "I never had a better foreman, Driver. You're a good man. But I will observe you seem mighty skittish lately. You've lost your grip on that bad temper, and I don't approve of it. I'm expecting you to work with the crew, not fight 'em. That applies to Charterhouse—if he takes my offer."

"I don't hone to stir up bad blood on a ranch," said Charterhouse thoughtfully.

Nickum shrugged his shoulders. "You're the doctor. But I'll suggest something. You've got a Shander horse under you, and he's apt to make a charge of stealing out of it, just to provoke a fight. You'd better keep your skirts clean. Ride into Angels with me and turn the brute over to Studd. I'll stand you to another animal."

"Angels ain't such a safe place for you, considering Shander's intentions."

Nickum doubled his fist. "The yellow dog ain't got the brass to fight me in the daylight! I'll ride into Angels— and out of it again!"

"Let's go, then," said Charterhouse and put his pony on the trail. Haggerty paired off with Nickum quickly, as if to stop further talk between the two, and this move brought Seastrom back beside Charterhouse. So they rode on along the open country and down the slope toward Casabella's county seat. Seastrom grinned frankly at Charterhouse and offered his hand.

"I will remark there ain't nobody I'd rather ride with," he murmured. "All I'm asking is that when the trouble busts, as it will sure's little green apples grow into big red ones, that you'll call your shots. No use both of us breaking the same gent's neck."

Charterhouse accepted the hand, smiling back. It was impossible to resist the rugged, irrepressible humor of Heck Seastrom. "Reckon you're training on a bigger rock since Manners hefted the other," he suggested.

"I'm through," chuckled Seastrom. "Saving my energy for bigger sport. But—" and he cut off further talk with a slight wave of the hand, indicating the men in front knowingly. Haggerty turned in the saddle to look forebodingly at them. Seastrom spoke with a tantalizing solicitude. "It's all right, Driver. We're watching the back trail. If any bold, bad man shows up, I'll tell you when to flop on your belly."

A flare of black hate deepened the vindictive ugliness of the foreman's face. He seemed about to let himself go but finally jerked about and rode on in glowering silence. Seastrom winked at Charterhouse and passed a finger across his throat significantly. The huddled buildings of

Angels appeared as they turned a shoulder of the ridge; they straightened for it and presently were entering the plaza, a plaza swimming with the increase of heat and devoid of life. Nickum led across to Nero Studd's and dismounted.

"Buck Manners is supposed to meet me here," he explained. "Guess he's late. Let's go in and get this horse business settled."

Studd was at a table, playing listless poker with four others. Nickum strode over. "Nero, Charterhouse had to borrow a pony off Shander the other night. He's leaving it in your stable."

"With my best personal regards to Mister Shander," drawled Charterhouse. "Due to intentions of hospitality he kept the one you lent me. You fellows can swap."

"Let Charterhouse have a pony out of your stable," directed Nickum. "On my account."

"Anything to please," agreed Studd and rose from the game. "Have a drink on me, boys. Heard about this horse business already."

"As how?" asked Charterhouse.

Studd lifted his immense shoulders. "It ain't my opinion, understand. It's only what I hear. Shander considered his horse was stolen and swore out a warrant for Sheriff Wolfert to execute."

"Let Wolfert try to trump a charge against a Box M man," said Nickum, all the fighting iron of his nature hardening the dogged face.

"Guess nobody knew he'd become one of your riders," suggested Studd, passing a bottle over the bar. "Don't think unkindly of me just because I broke the bad news to you. I know where my bread's buttered and I sure hope I never see the day when Box M is challenged. Empty the bottle. I'll run across and see about getting a horse."

They saw his burly frame cruise deliberately over the shade of the porch and on into the drenching sunlight of the open plaza. The saloon droned and those loitering men at the tables handled their cards with a futile laziness that was oppressive. Haggerty drank a second glass with a touch of nervousness and kept looking out upon the street. Seastrom chuckled.

"Something sort of reminds me of trouble smoking up."

"Never knew a yellow dog yet that would stand and fight," said Nickum. "We'll just stick around and find out if Wolfert wants to make an issue of this. I'd be pleased to have him declare his intentions."

Meanwhile Nero Studd strode through the stable, only checking his pace to throw an order at the roustabout. "Put a saddle on the claybank, and I'll be back for it." Going through the rear door, he swung to the right and walked the breadth of three buildings. Knocking briefly at the door of the fourth, he went into a small back room. Beef Graney and Sheriff Ike Wolfert were standing in it and shifted expectantly.

"What's on old John's mind?" asked Wolfert.

"He's took Charterhouse as a rider," said Studd. "That makes it bad. Gosh only knows how much Charterhouse learned at Shander's last night, or how much he's told Nickum. Looks to me as if our chance of getting the stranger out of the way is some slimmer. Would of been easy. Now that Nickum's back of him it ain't."

"That's why I ducked in here when I saw 'em ride up," said Wolfert. "I'll be boiled in grease afore I try to serve a warrant in front of Nickum. Damn Shander! Why'd he let Charterhouse get away?"

Graney's beefy cheeks stiffened. "Studd, there won't be any better time than now. You get me? Here they are, a long ways from help. No use of trying to smile it out. Nickum must have got warning about the ambush. There's some of Charterhouse's work, I'm betting. Well, why not do it now? Don't forget that—"

Studd held up a warning arm. "Don't mention any names, Graney. Not even to yourself. Dangerous. But your idea is good. And we can use Charterhouse's stolen horse to rig the business up right. Wolfert, you go around town, keeping out of sight, and drum up five or six boys. Post 'em around the saloon where they won't be seen. One in the stable. Another in front of Madame LeSeur's. I'll ease back to the saloon with a horse I promised Charterhouse and stick there. Graney, you go down and saddle up Charterhouse's original animal and ride into sight. Charterhouse will jump you about it in a minute. You produce a bill of sale—write one now and sign anybody's you want. He'll argue about it and then it is just a matter of what happens next. That clear?"

Graney nodded. "Suits me. I'll take care of Charterhouse. But you be damned sure the others are blocked off and shot down."

Wolfert stirred uneasily. "What am I to do?"

"Come in a little ahead of Graney," decided Studd, "and argue with old John. When the shooting starts, just let him have it."

"How about Seastrom?"

Studd's stolid countenance turned almost sly. "Who would you suppose would finish the Swede? Use your head. All right, I'm going back. Give yourself fifteen minutes, Graney. Wolfert, you get busy now." He backed out of the room and returned through the stable, catching up the horse the roustabout had saddled. He left it in front of his saloon and entered. Upon the impassive, swarthy skin was not even a flimsy trace of the death sentence he had improvised and so shortly would add another weltering, grim chapter to a town already old in violence.

A faint beam of friendliness struggled through Studd's murky eyes, and the same heavy joviality was in his voice when he returned to the saloon.

"I'm giving you the claybank this time, Charterhouse. A stout horse. And, by the way, I'll pay off on your stolen rig whenever you say the word. I figured it was my fault in a way. Have another drink." Passing down the room, his foot struck a chair and he grumbled at the indolent players. "You boys have roosted here long enough. Go sleep some place else for a change."

Charterhouse, swift to detect subtle changes of human temperature, felt some strange current pass through the saloon. The men at the table rose and sauntered through the front door, leaving Studd's empty excepting for the saloonkeeper and the Box M quartet. Neither Nickum nor Haggerty appeared to draw out of their own thoughts, but

Seastrom's flash of humor grew more brilliant and he dropped an eyelid to Charterhouse.

"Well, what next?"

Nickum pushed away the bottle. "Where's Wolfert?"

"Snoozing somewhere, I guess," said Studd. "No, here he comes now. Ike, step in."

Wolfert veered from the walk and stopped on the threshold. "Yeah? Hello, Nickum. Thought I heard—"

Nickum cut in brusquely. "I hear you carry a warrant for horse stealing."

Wolfert licked his lips. "That's right. Shander swore it for this gentleman—" indicating Charterhouse— "bright and early this morning."

"Going to serve it?"

"Well, John, you know I got to do what the law requires. No option on my part. I didn't swear out the warrant. I'm only sworn to carry out my duty."

Nickum snorted. "Taking your duty pretty serious lately, ain't you, Wolfert?"

"Don't like to hear you make insinuations," muttered Wolfert. "I have done my level best to cater to Box M. You got no call to say I ain't reasonable thataway."

"Charterhouse is under Box M protection," stated Nickum bluntly. "Your warrant is just a piece of paper, nothing more. Wouldn't advise you to draw it on him today or any other time."

"You're sure leaving me in a bad place, John. What'll Shander say?"

"Let him cook up another lie better'n this one. It's so rotten it stinks."

"That ain't for me to say," was Wolfert's surly response. "I ain't the judge."

Charterhouse stepped carefully away from the bar and pointed through the door. "What's the gentleman's name who's so polite as to ride my horse to town?"

"Graney, by golly," muttered Seastrom. And dead silence fell over the room. Graney rode into the saloon rack and slid idly to the ground. The black hide of Charterhouse's mount glistened under the sun and the silver corners of the fine acorn leaf saddle flashed brilliantly.

Charterhouse turned back to the group, graven-cheeked. His skin crawled with the shock of electric excitement; for the second time he found himself trying to penetrate Nero Studd's poker expression. Of the whole party, Haggerty alone seemed to display honest surprise. The foreman shifted uneasily, looking from the door back to Nickum and thence to Studd. Seastrom was rubbing the palms of his hands along the bar, producing a small squeaking sound that seemed to irritate both Haggerty and Wolfert. Both of them glowered at Seastrom, whereupon he laughed and broke the tension.

"Your horse?" challenged Nickum.

"Mine," drawled Charterhouse.

Graney had turned away from the rack and was walking off. Charterhouse, without haste, strolled out of the door and hailed the man, feeling the others come crowding after him.

"Just a minute, partner. You've got a piece of nice horseflesh there."

Graney whirled, almost too swiftly. Charterhouse's elbows crooked and stopped. Graney threw his own hands wide of his hips and growled, "Sure I have, and what of it?"

It was a pretty raw rig, Charterhouse reflected. A pretty crude way to bring on a scrap. Looking at the profusely sweating Graney, he wondered just how the cards lay. A man had popped into sight by the stable; and the men behind him were shifting. He wanted to turn and see where Studd and Wolfert were standing but didn't dare.

"Naturally," went on Charterhouse, slurring the words, "you've got a bill of sale for this gear?"

"Correct. I take a receipt for my money. If you stick around Casabella very long, you'll get that habit, too."

"A-huh. Well, let's see this bill of sale."

"What for?" demanded Graney, coming closer.

"You know the answer as well as I do," murmured Charterhouse. "But in order to play up to your game, I'll mention this is my horse and rig."

"Might have been. Ain't now."

"Beg to differ."

Graney went into his coat pocket and affected to have trouble finding a slip of paper that he finally flourished. Charterhouse took it and saw a formal bill of sale from one Ramon de Rio, signed with considerable of a flourish.

"Yeah. Legal and everything," drawled Charterhouse. "Who is this Ramon de Rio?"

Seastrom's amused reply cut over Charterhouse's shoulder. "That one, huh? Well, Beef, you sure picked a good one. Ramon's dead up in the rocks of Red Draw. He missed his shot at Nickum."

Charterhouse felt the effect of that statement. It audibly disturbed those back of him. Beef Graney dashed the sweat out of his eyes with a round oath. "What's that got to do with me? I paid for that horse. Yeah, I know it used to be yours, Charterhouse. Ramon bought it from you in town yesterday."

"Oh, you've got it worked out that complete?" said Charterhouse. "Too bad. It ain't the true facts, even if Ramon said so, which I'm inclined some to doubt."

"Be careful of your words," Graney warned him. "You'll stand accountable for them."

"Willing to," averred Charterhouse. "Now the next move seems to be up to me. Which I will make, according to rule. This is my horse. It always was, and it always will be. You've had your little ride in a white man's saddle and that's all you'll get."

"Stay away from that horse, Charterhouse!"

"Boys," broke in Wolfert. "I'll have no shooting around Angels. Take your troubles to the judge."

"Very noble," applauded Charterhouse. "Sorry I can't look around to congratulate your sentiments. Mister Graney, I intend to step slowly back to the horse, take the reins, and step aboard."

"When you touch the ribbons, you'll have to draw!" snapped Graney and tried again to clear the sweat out of his eyes. Charterhouse took a backward pace and halted. A rider came posting into Angels from the east, kicking up a high cloud of plaza dust. He cut across to the saloon and sprang down before the pony had completely stopped —Buck Manners. He showed his usual cheerful manner, but it was instantly repressed at sight of Graney and Charterhouse confronting each other so cagily.

"Now what?"

"A little dicker about horses," called Nickum. "Stay aside, Buck."

Manners scanned the plaza with a quick glance. "Listen, why fight? Let's get these fellows to talk it over and come to a peaceful—"

"Stay aside, Buck," repeated Nickum gruffly. "I'm waiting to see if a yellow dog will actually fight in the open. Get off your horse before somebody takes you for a target."

Manners stared at Graney. "You sure that's *your* horse, Beef?"

"I said it," retorted Graney, "and I ain't backing down now."

"All right. No objections from me. A free and open fight. Leave 'em alone, everybody." There was a rising ring of authority in his words. "Get out of range, Wolfert, you dummy."

"Say, Manners—"

"Shut up. If it's going to be a fight, I'll help see it's on the level."

"You touch that horse, Charterhouse," repeated Graney, furrows of worry coming to his forehead, "and you take a slug."

Charterhouse stepped deliberately back and whipped the dangling reins with his left hand, letting them drop the following instant. He had called Graney's bluff and across the interval he saw the heavy fellow's face, dripping wet, swing slowly from side to side, containing a mixture of puzzlement and anger. Quite obviously he had missed the fighting moment; during the delay he appeared to be struggling with unforeseen circumstances and trying to adjust himself to them. The crowd stood rooted, without a sound; Charterhouse never let his attention stray. Graney's eyes burned against him, increasingly intent, and Graney's body was pitched a little forward as if ready to send all his muscles into a mighty effort. Then Buck Manners laughed outright and said ironically, "Somebody get a camera and snap this comic opera. Charterhouse—"

Charterhouse turned his head slightly to catch Manners' face. Graney moved. His palm slapped against leather in the utter stillness. His rounding body plunged aside with the lift and explosion of his gun. Charterhouse, never moving out of his tracks, worked with the smoothness of an automatic machine and hardly was conscious of his draw until the smash of his own revolver beat against him and his wrist kicked back with the weapon's recoil. Graney stiffened, all his chubby face beaded in big globes of sweat; a leer of pain stamped his lips, but there was again the roar of a shot, and as the echo of it rocketed away into the droning heat of Angels, Graney emitted a cracked, forlorn cry and dropped straight down. Charterhouse heard him mutter, "Manners!" and that was all.

The tendrils of gun smoke eddied into Charterhouse's nostrils. Swinging toward Manners he spoke in a dry, distant voice that seemed not his own. "Was you aiming to take my attention away from Graney when he was about to draw?"

Manners stared at the dead man with an unusual soberness. "Don't be a damned fool, Charterhouse. I wanted you to put up your gun. I would have covered him myself while we talked the business over. He knew he was on the poor end of the bluff and I don't think he wanted to go through with it. Sorry for the fellow, but it was his own making."

Charterhouse turned around. Seastrom and old John Nickum were standing shoulder to shoulder against the saloon wall. Haggerty was also against the wall but slightly removed from them. On the outer edge of the walk Studd and Wolfert were posted; so the opposing parties stood, saying nothing, watching for anything. At the far end of the street a man came suddenly around a building with a rifle half lifted and ducked back. Charterhouse challenged Wolfert.

"Any inclination to serve that warrant on me, Sheriff?"

"I'm trying to get along with you men," muttered Wolfert. "Don't make it hard for me. I ain't tried to serve no warrant, have I? Blamed if I don't think I'll turn in my star. Public official in this county just gets kicked from corner to corner. No thanks and plumb little pay."

Old John Nickum shot a coldly triumphant glance at Wolfert and Studd. "Why don't you go through with it? What's stopping you?"

"Through with what?" Studd wanted to know.

"Don't fake with me," snorted Nickum. "You had a killing ribbed up. I'm too old not to understand the signs. You boys are pretty crude in your ways. What's all those men posted around for? Reckon I ain't seen 'em waiting to get a fair shot? Hell, Studd, you're clumsy. Graney was the only one with guts enough to go through with his play. None of you others had sand enough to back him up."

"You still got me wrong," complained Studd and spread his broad paws outward.

"Looks to me," broke in Manners, "as if I was going to have to station about twenty of my men in this town to keep it straight. If you can't keep order, Wolfert, you'd better resign. It's a poor day when Angels turns against Box M. I've tried to maintain a fair and open place with the whole county, but I will not stand by and see John Nickum injured. First thing you know, Box M will come into Angels and give it a clean-up."

"Yellow dogs never fight in the open," boomed Nickum. "Come to the hotel, Buck, and let's transact our business."

The two of them strolled over to Madame LeSeur's. Twenty minutes later they came out again. Nickum found his party waiting for him in the shade of the stable.

"If the offer is still open," said Charterhouse, "I'll be glad to ride for Box M."

Nickum surveyed Charterhouse with manifest approval. "You bet the offer is open. I know a fighter when I see one. Let's go."

The four of them strung out of Angels leisurely. Haggerty was again paired off with the boss, sour face clamped around a chew of tobacco, never speaking and never looking aside. Seastrom chuckled and winked at Charterhouse.

"Brother, you looked hard when you fronted Mister Graney. What I mean is you looked hard."

"Over and done with," said Charterhouse soberly.

"Better get that out of your coco. The ball's just started. And it will be hell on greased wheels. Casabella goes crazy at the smell of a little blood.

Chapter FIVE

Speech came droning softly through the padded desert darkness as the rulers of Casabella met and planned on the open range. A horse blubbered and another chewed on its bit. Men in the saddle made a dim ring under faint crystals of starlight. A wind blew gently out of the lonely horizons.

"We misplayed our hand twice and unless we make the right move next time, we'll pay for our fun. You boys hear me? I think Charterhouse was responsible for tipping off the ambush. Since the Mexican died on his belly without firing a shot, we won't ever know the truth of the matter, but my guess is Charterhouse knew all about it. I'm telling you fellows, Charterhouse is built to fight. I saw him make his draw, and it was as pretty as I've looked at since Slinger Hogan cashed in. He's got the same wrist break Hogan had and he didn't try to jump out of his skin like Graney. Graney was fast but he didn't have the guts to stand in his tracks and that's what killed him."

"We'll get Charterhouse," said Studd's heavy voice.

"You'd better. He's no fool pilgrim. He knew that fight was all rigged. And he'll step around like a cat. I don't fancy having that lean, long drink of water on my trail. He's soft talking but he's got hazel eyes. And I never met a hazel-eyed man yet that wasn't a blazing killer when he went on a rampage. I'm telling you, the cards have got to be played right from this time on. No more fooling. We made enough mistakes to hang."

"Ain't my fault," growled Studd. "We'd of got Nickum this day if we'd been let alone. He's just as wise as Charterhouse. They both know plenty. And Nickum's got to fall before he spreads his information at large."

"Talk, talk," broke in another. This was Wolfert, words

67

breaking nervously. "All we do is talk about things we had ought to do or things we tried to do and boggled. I'm beginning to think we're sunk."

"Oh, shut up. You've had the willies ever since Nickum's kid took your slug—"

"Stop that! Want to advertise to the whole cursed county who got him?"

"Studd."

"Yeah, Shander?"

"I want you to get hold of the influential Mexican men. That's easy for you, considering you've played their political game all these years. Tell them to pass on the word to all their friends and dependents to watch for Box M riders by day or night, and send word to you. Get the grapevine system working. Nickum plays this game as well as we do and it'd be like him to storm down and wipe somebody off the map. Tell the Mexicans to keep watch."

"You bet Nickum plays the same kind of poker," put in Wolfert. "Ever stop to think that it's as easy for one of us to get ambushed as for them?"

"This is war, Wolfert. If you're afraid, crawl out."

"And get shot in the back for crawling?" said Wolfert bitterly. "I know where I stand."

"Glad you do," muttered Studd. "I been wondering about that. But we ain't made any reasonable plans yet about Charterhouse and Nickum. I'm repeating—they got to go soon. You dally this thing along, Shander, and we'll be licked before we start."

"Curly, I've got a job for you," Shander said, ignoring Studd's comment.

A rather thin, uneven voice joined in. "Yeah, I been waiting for something to do. My outfit's awful tired of Dead Man Range."

"Take three of your best shots and coolest heads, better pick old-timers in your bunch. Put one up in the timber by the Bowlus place. Another between Box M and Fort Carson. Have the third get as close to Box M on the north as he can possibly find concealment. And they are to stick it out until they get a bullet into either Nickum or Charterhouse. Meanwhile, I think we'll rig up a bigger bit of

fun. Keep your men collected, Curly, and wait for a signal
from me. If I locate a part of Nickum's men starting off to
look for beef, I'll get word to you. The rest is your business. One way or another we'll whipsaw Nickum into
proper shape to hit him. That's definite enough. The biggest thing is to hang back and wait for the breaks. But I
want this prairie patrolled at night; and I want Box M
watched by day. It will only be a matter of forty-eight
hours before something drops."

"Don't sound active enough to me," observed Studd.

"No? What more do you want? We've got our men posted at four different places. We've got a system to get information to us. Once we get information, we can collect
our strength and throw it anywhere within three hours'
riding. Here's something else. Camp a man at Fort Carson, Curly. And another five miles nearer Box M. Everybody get that. If there's word to be relayed to any of us,
these fellows pass it on. I guess we've got this organized
now. Somebody's posted conveniently all around Box M.
They can't move without our seeing it. And what we can't
learn from the outside, I think we'll learn from inside
sources."

"Speaking of which, Shander," broke in Wolfert, "It
seems to me your trusting—"

"Mention no names, Wolfert. I know what I'm doing.
The man you speak about is all right. He's in a damned
dangerous position and he's got to go slow."

"We'll have to show results in forty-eight hours or fold
up," insisted Studd.

"We will. Remember the shot signals. Be sure all your
riders know them, and know how to answer them. Finally,
if it comes to a matter of a pitched battle, I want everybody to be on their toes so that each outfit can be ready to
move on a minute's notice. That's why I want all the
scouts posted. If Nickum should elect to move out with
his whole bunch and start destroying, we have all got to
be in shape to come down on top of him. That means every man has got to be within easy two or three hours' ride
from any place around here. That's all. Get off and keep
your mouths shut."

"I wish I was sure——" began Wolfert, and was suppressed by a rough retort.

"Nobody's sure of anything till he's dead. Some of us may be dead by next sundown. Nobody knows. But I'm telling you all that this spread is the biggest prize in the west, once we lay hands on it. Make rich men of all of us. Because with Nickum gone the power in the county goes to us, and we take all the offices, levy toll on every other big rancher, and in general we will be in shape to have anything worth having in Casabella. Any objections to that?"

A sardonic answer emerged from a more distant part of the circle. "Sounds fine, providing some of us don't try to hog the prize entire. Such things happen."

"Wait till that time comes. Hang together or hang separate. We're in too deep to start quarreling now."

"Thieves always quarrel," said the sardonic one. "We will, too, when we get our fingers in the pie. But what of it? If we wasn't raising one kind of hell and deceit, we'd be doing it in another way. Casabella politics. Nobody's ever satisfied with nothing. We never get our belly full of scrapping and we never get enough plunder. Well, it don't matter. Let's go."

The ring dissolved and riders hurried off in different directions. Silence fell; the whispered treacheries of human kind faded into the great, ageless mystery of the shadow-cloaked earth and the dim, frosted stars looked down indifferently.

Chapter SIX

Old John Nickum, bearing in mind the recent attacks made on him, took a wide swing over the desert with Clint Charterhouse to inspect a bunch of his cattle in the northwest; having done that, he discovered fresh hoof-prints along the trail and these he followed until they petered out in the hardpan bottom of an arroyo, driving east toward Dead Man's Range. Therefore, it was not until near dusk that Charterhouse got his first sight of Box M home quarters. The first landmark was a high windmill tower standing up between rows of trees; successively the party flanked corral wings, an ice house, several sodded storerooms, an enormous shed for haying implements and wagons, a still more enormous barn, three long bunk-houses built like boxcars, and finally the main house which was constructed in a fashion common to the southern cattle country.

One rambling wing was divided into rooms, each room letting out separately upon a covered porch running the whole length of the place. Lights gleamed pleasantly through an open door, and the fragrance of lilacs hung over the yard. Seastrom and Haggerty turned off and Charterhouse was about to follow them when Nickum interrupted. "You'll be one of the boys soon enough. Consider yourself a guest tonight." A queer, shrunken figure ambled up and took their horses as they dismounted and went up the porch. Nickum led Charterhouse along to a farther door, opened it and stepped through to light a lamp.

"Your room until we get a place for you in the bunk-house tomorrow. Wash up and come to the main room."

"Not good business for a new hand like me to assume

privileges over the crew," observed Charterhouse thoughtfully.

But Nickum, half down the porch, answered gruffly. "It's my pleasure to find guests worth having. I am beholden to you, which is sufficient for me and will be sufficient for all Box M. Allow me to be the judge in my own house."

Alone, Charterhouse surveyed the neat little bedroom with a strange revival of memories long slumbering. The clean plastered walls, the patchwork spread on the bed, the faint smell of lavender brought back a remote childhood. In such a room he once had lived, long, long ago. Here was the peace of family life, here was the impress of some gentle hand reminding him of his own hard, solitary life through all the intervening years. Pouring water into a china basin, he suddenly recalled Sherry Nickum.

Fire had flashed at their meeting; it might flash again. There was nothing flimsy about her. She was old John Nickum's daughter, owning the strong Nickum temper—a girl of the prairie and moulded by its influences. He recalled clearly the picture she made standing in the doorway of blind Bowlus' cabin, slim and stiff, the lazy eyes hot with anger, copper hair shining in the fresh sun.

A bell sounded over the quiet yard. Charterhouse shook the dust out of his coat and passed out to the porch. Men filed around the house with the murmur of their talk sounding peacefully in the dusk. Cigarette tips glittered, the soft wind brushed through the poplar tops. Charterhouse sighed and squared himself at the main door. Nickum waited inside for him and he saw Sherry in a dawn pink dress standing lithe and graceful by a chair; her arms and throat had an ivory beauty and the mass of auburn hair gave her a height and serenity that for the moment utterly destroyed his self-possession. He crossed the threshold and soberly met her glance. Nickum turned.

"Charterhouse—my daughter, Sherry. This is the boy, Sherry, to whom I owe an obligation."

She stepped forward and he felt the pressure of her firm palm in his own calloused fist. A deeper rose dyed her cheeks, the gray and lazy eyes lighted with an inner humor. "I am prepared to forgive—and be forgiven," she murmured. "Welcome to our home, Clint Charterhouse."

"Met before?" queried Nickum, puzzled.

"At Bowlus'," said the girl, mouth curling into a smile. "I warned him to get off Box M."

"Nobody can say you ain't had ample warning, Charterhouse," chuckled Nickum. "We will try to be more friendly hereafter. Let's eat." He went ahead into a small dining room. Sherry walked beside Charterhouse, looking up at him."

"Am I forgiven? You haven't said."

"I would be a presuming man," replied Charterhouse, "if I admitted you needed my forgiveness."

"Spoken gallantly," she said very gaily. "But you didn't feel that way about it this morning."

That made him grin, the fine lines crinkling about his eyes; and the bronzed, thoughtful features lightened tremendously. "I think we both had our Irish up then," he drawled. "You and I seem to have a temper."

"Yes," and she shot a quick look at him, "but I hope we are not going to fight any more."

"Never," said Clint so strongly that her color deepened again. He waited at her chair until she was seated, then went around to his own. A hum of talk came through from the crew's dining room. Heck Seastrom was arguing about something with his characteristic headlong vigor. "I like that chap," went on Clint.

"Seastrom?" grunted Nickum. "Oh, he's all right. Wastes a lot of energy and gets into more jackpots than all the rest of the bunch put together."

"That's why I like him. Used to ride with a partner built just about Seastrom's style. Always got into a lot of horseplay, but when trouble started he was johnny on the spot. And when trouble finished he was still among those present. A long time ago."

"Now that sounded forlorn and sad," observed Sherry. "Has your life been so checkered?"

He chuckled. "Oh, I'm no tragic figure with a black past. But I sort of felt down when I rode up to your place. It got me to thinking about where I was born and raised and how long it had been since I last slept in a civilized room and ate at a table with a white cloth and silver. I weaned early and have been used to roundup fare ever since. This is a treat. I don't reckon you folks know just how much of a treat it is."

"I can guess," said Sherry. A shadow crossed her clear face. "It is nice to have someone sitting in your chair again. My brother sat there up until a few months ago. He—" very slowly, "was killed from ambush."

Nickum's ruddy cheeks grew tight. "At the same spot they tried to get me. Well, the day will come. No man can survive a hundred chances."

"Dad!"

But Nickum shook his head. "Got to be straight about it, Sherry. If they want me bad enough, they'll get me. I've felt it in my bones a long while. Only one way to beat that gang. Smash 'em before they get out of their tracks."

"That being the case," reflected Clint, "I don't believe I'd hesitate as to choice."

"First sensible opinion anybody's given me for a long time," said Nickum and looked more fully at Clint. "You're right. Buck Manners is wrong. This shilly-shally only gives Shander more time to tighten his lines and spread his poison. Buck's afraid to face the idea of a general war, afraid he won't sleep good at night for having helped bring one on. I'll admit it's hard and a cruel business. But Casabella's always been a hard and cruel county. Lawless, full of cutthroats, full of slippery politicians. I've battled 'em all my life. Now it's either a showdown—their blood or my blood. I don't propose to die, and I don't propose to see Box M pass into other hands. When that happens, Casabella won't be fit for hogs to root in."

"Buck is on your side, don't forget that," Sherry reminded him.

"Sure, sure. But he's trying to spread too much oil, spraddle too many fences. He thinks we can talk a way out of this trouble. If he was thirty years older, he'd know different. Right now Shander and Curly ain't touching his ranch. They want him to feel like everything's all right and that I'm too excitable. But once they get me, Buck Manners won't last half an hour. He don't realize he's playing into their hands that way. Charterhouse, where'd you learn to play Indian, anyhow? You took care of yourself pretty well in the last forty-eight hours."

"Matter of horse sense, I reckon," mused Clint.

"We need more horse sense in this country," growled Nickum. "You took the initiative and did something on your own account, which is more than any of my men would do. They'll follow well but they can't lead worth a damn. I can't be everywhere at once and I can't smell down tracks like I used to. Can't ride as long and as hard, either. You willing to be a lieutenant around here?"

"How about Haggerty?"

Sherry frowned. "I wish he was some place else," she broke in.

"He's a good prod for the men," countered Nickum. "I'd like him better if he controlled his temper. Never mind Haggerty. He will do what I tell him and if he doesn't like taking orders from you—which it will amount to—then he must go. I am offering you plenty of room and responsibility."

"You don't know much about me," reflected Clint.

"I'll stand on my judgment," declared Nickum.

Clint found the girl watching him with a trace of anxiety. Her white hands rested quite still on the table and her rounding lips were pursed together. He thought he saw sudden warmth in the gray eyes; and whatever cautions and qualifications might have been in his head, they dissolved then and there.

"Take it," he decided laconically.

Father and daughter looked at each other. Nickum cleared his throat two or three times irritably. "Don't mind saying that lifts a load off my shoulders, Charterhouse. You will consider that room your own, this table your proper place, and the house open to you at all times."

The girl smiled brilliantly. They rose and went back to the living room; night chill already had come through the house, and Sherry touched a match to the fireplace. Clint ranged beside it with a sense of comfort sweeping over him like some powerful drug. After all the long years of drifting about, anchorless and alone, he felt as if he were at last home. The room, its lights and shadows and its high beams, took on a strange familiarity. Sherry Nickum smiled up at him, murmuring, "You are a very solemn man sometimes, Clint Charterhouse. You were looking far off, far ahead then. What did you see?"

He shook his head, the fine feeling partly fading away. This was the girl who had sworn herself to another man; all that beauty and vigor and gay spirits were for Buck Manners.

"I wish I could say I saw something," he said, still sober, "but I guess I was just looking at blank space."

"Depends," was Sherry's very soft answer.

Nickum roused himself and lowered his pipe. "I'll collect the boys in the morning and explain your place among—"

A horse clattered across the yard's packed earth and a rowdy hail shot through the door. "Put another log on the fire—here comes a fella!"

Buck Manners appeared in the doorway, hat off, yellow hair tousled and a broad smile on the magnetic face. Charterhouse thought a part of the smile sank away when Manners saw him there; and certainly there was a swift and broadening flare of interest in the man's eyes. But he spoke casually around the circle.

"Nickum—hello again. Sherry, you look like something just this minute out of a picture. How, Charterhouse. Glad to see you again. John put the Box M brand on you?"

"Yeah," agreed Clint. "So short a time ago you can smell scorched skin."

"Thought you'd been rope-burned and scary," remarked Manners, adjusting himself indolently in a fat easy chair. He rolled a cigarette, eyes passing between Charterhouse and the girl with quick, decisive flashes.

"I guess I've been gentled," drawled Clint. He met the rollicking ranchman's blue eyes and found himself wondering at the hard, observant brightness that appeared and disappeared within the surface humor. He had already matched strength with Manners; the man was a fighter, for all his easy-going ways. It was difficult to tell at what point he would switch from careless indifference to tremendous strength.

"Well, you'll never wear a better brand," decided Manners. And added a lazy afterthought. "No matter how many others you may have worn before."

Clint asked himself a silent question. "What's the snapper to that, I wonder. Might be just an observation, Might be a dig."

Sherry broke in. "You've just missed supper, Buck. I'll sit at the table with you, though."

"Thanks no. Ate early. Only figure to stay for a spell. These days I don't like to pull away from the ranch for too long. Never know what's going to happen next. By the way, John, I wanted to pass on a piece of information you might use. Curly's shifted his territory. He's grazing over in Dead Man lately. I've seen campfires there the last few nights; also have heard a few stray noises passing my place when honest folk sleep."

"Moving closer to me," was Nickum's grim remark. "The wolves slink in and wait for a chance. I wonder how many tough nuts he's got, Buck?"

"Ten-fifteen, I suppose," judged Manners, watching his cigarette smoke curl to the ceiling. "Maybe more. Charterhouse, you may have a better guess."

"As how?" Clint demanded.

"Well, you were at Shander's last night and got some dope, didn't you?"

"Mostly I was worrying about getting away. Curly was there with some of his men, though. How many, I couldn't say, for part of the bunch might have been Shander's own riders."

"Shander don't carry a big outfit. Only about twelve-fourteen hands."

"This Curly," went on Charterhouse, "is a fool for being proud of himself. If I was a brush jumper, I'd keep my face hid. He took the pains to introduce himself to me, saying he wanted me to know him next time we met."

"That's Curly's weakness, all right," grinned Manners. "He likes to grandstand. But don't figure him any the less wild for that trick. He's a white savage. Shoot you back or front, makes no difference to him."

"I judged that," mused Clint, whereat Manners studied him again through the smoke.

Sherry, standing so quietly by the fire, had observed all these silent interchanges with soberly pursed lips. Being thoroughly feminine, she had compared them from the moment they faced each other; a tall, laughing man with yellow hair and a reckless exuberance of spirit placed beside an equally tall man whose smile was slow and seldom and whose features were bronzed, almost gaunt. One found life a great game and pursued it with zest; the other had traveled a lonely trail. The sun and the rain, the burning heat and the knife slash of the blizzard had whipped him down to flat sinews and fashioned him so that even here in the room he could not drop the trick of appearing to look far across the horizons.

"Just wanted to tell you that for your own information, John," pursued Manners. "Any plans?"

"I will sleep on it," said Nickum. "If I feel in the morning as I feel now, the war is on. They have tried twice for me. I reckon that's excuse enough to tame Casabella. Ten years ago I wouldn't have needed the sleep. I'd be in the saddle now. When a man gets older, he seems to take longer stock."

"You've got my outfit to draw on any time you see fit," Manners told him.

"Thanks. My outfit is big enough. All I have been needing is one man able to plunge ahead and use his own head while he fights. I've got him now, I think. This boy here—" pointing to Charterhouse. "Consider him as a member of the family, Buck."

Manners lifted his head, plainly surprised. "Member of the family?"

Sherry flushed visibly. Nickum filled his pipe. "I mean that from now on you're to consider him second man around here. If he asks you for help or advice, I want you should consider it the same as if I personally asked it."

"Gladly," agreed Manners, the word sounding rather dry. "I'll say, however, that I have been offering myself for that sort of work a great many months before Charterhouse came along. As a prospective member of the family—" grinning at Sherry, "what's wrong with my good right arm?"

Nickum chose his words very carefully, tamping down his tobacco. "I've known you since you were a kid, Buck. Life never was very hard on you. Everything come easy, go easy. You like to keep on even terms with folks, you like to play peacemaker. You never had to fight crooks on their own terms. I'm welcoming you as a son-in-law gladly. Don't doubt it. But you ain't a bloodhound. Take Charterhouse here. He fell into trouble the minute he hit Angels. I bit him in the ear. So did Haggerty. Had his horse stolen. Shander grabbed him and tried to keep him.

"He shoots his way out of that, puts two and two together and trails all over hell's half acre, climbs a tree, smells out that Mexican ambushed to get me and pots him cold. Then comes to Angels and accepts a ribbed fight and downs Graney. No uncomplimentary comparisons, Buck, but Charterhouse was born with a nose for trouble and seems to have been raised to all the bitter tricks. That's the man I need. He's had my sort of a life—the only kind of a life that will pay dividends in fighting Shander."

Manners rose, laughing shortly. "I know I was born with a gold spoon, John, but it hurts to have it put so plainly. I'm not grousing. I know the fellow's good. He muscled me down, and by Judas, that means he's blamed good. I'll cooperate with him any time. That goes, Charterhouse. But I still may be useful. When you get ready to crush 'em, let me join in."

"You're not going so soon," protested the girl.

"Really must get back," said Manners. He put out his hand to Charterhouse. "Good luck, old horse."

"Thanks," drawled Charterhouse. "Don't consider me as high as Nickum does."

"He seldom ever makes a mistake," replied Manners. "I

hope he isn't making one now. Sherry, my love, good night and I wish you didn't look so blessed pretty with a handsome young fellow like Charterhouse around. I may lose all my advantage with you."

The color of her face deepened but she flashed a mischievous glance between them. "I doubt if you need worry Buck. It is my impression that Clint Charterhouse has never looked at a woman twice."

"I wish I could depend on it," retorted Manners, "but there's something wrong with his eyes if he doesn't look at you twice."

The two of them went to the porch. Charterhouse heard a low chuckle and a tinkling laugh and then the beat of hoofs traveling swiftly out. He stared into the fire somberly. There was nothing wrong with his eyes, he reflected, but it would save him heartbreak if he kept them away from Sherry Nickum.

She came back, sober and thoughtful. "Dad, I don't believe he relished your comparisons."

"Man's got to swallow the truth, sweet or bitter," granted Nickum.

Charterhouse spoke. "You have made an enemy for me."

"Buck?" grunted Nickum, astonished.

Charterhouse nodded. "Just so."

"Hell, that's a foolish idea," retorted Nickum. But Sherry caught Clint's eye and though he was no hand at reading unspoken thoughts, he knew she agreed with him. She put an arm to his elbow.

"Walk with me."

There was a shawl on a table by the door that she took up and whipped around her shoulders. They crossed the porch and strolled along the yard with the lights of the bunkhouses making yellow pathways across the earth. Water trickled near by, the trees were sighing with the wind and horses stamped patiently in the barn. The moon hung rakishly in a corner of the sky, pale against all the surrounding darkness; and memories kept returning to Clint.

"Like coming into shelter after a hard day outside," he

mused aloud. "I never knew anything could be so peaceful or quiet. Reckon I have missed a great deal so far."

"I'm glad to know you've found that missing element here," said she quietly.

"Found it, and will lose it again."

"Why so? You sound so wistful, as if there never was any real happiness possible for you."

"Don't make me out a man with a sorrowful past." he warned her. "I've just wandered along, nothing much behind and nothing much ahead."

"Then I was right when I told Buck you never cared to look at a woman twice?"

"Up till now," said Clint and fell silent.

"Somewhere," she murmured, "you learned how to speak gallantly."

They turned, swinging along another row of trees, crossed a ditch with her body swaying lightly against him and lightly away. He saw the pale silhouette of her face, dim and beautiful against the velvet curtin of this prairie night and was troubled with the faint fragrance of her hair.

"I brought you out," she continued after a long while, "to say that I am truly sorry for my temper this morning. I was uncertain, and I can never find any kindness in my heart for those men who killed my brother. But—we'll not quarrel like that again, Clint Charterhouse. As long as you stay here I want you to regard this as home. I'll feel happy if you do."

"Let's scratch my remarks off the record, too," he drawled. "I'd rather have your good wishes—"

There was no need of finishing the sentence. He let it trail into the shadows. Part of his attention, so long trained to watchfulness that it never wholly slept, kept striking back to a blurred poplar trunk near the house. He thought he had seen a slight shifting there. After they went over the ditch and circled the barn he lost sight of the tree; when he picked up a view of it again, the outline of the trunk was distinctly slimmer.

"I wanted to say something else as well," said the girl, finding more difficulty with her words. "You spoke of having made an enemy. I hate to say it, but I think you have. Buck is a fine, straight man. I know him better than anybody else, I think, and I've never known a more thorough gentleman. Yet Dad hurt him, even if he didn't show it through his smile. Buck is proud of his strength and proud of everything he owns. You don't know that side of him. I do. Now and then I catch flashes of it that are startling."

"I understand," said Clint. "When he wants a thing he wants it pretty bad and is willing to scrap for it. I take him to be a pretty able scrapper."

"Then you do see what I mean. He has never revealed himself, but I have often thought he would like to rule Casabella for the sense of power it would give him. To be able to justify all that energy and ability that he can't find an outlet for now. What I wanted to say was that you must, whatever else you do, be straight, frank and shoulder to shoulder with him. Promise me you'll never permit yourself to get into an argument with him. Promise me that."

"A large order," mused Clint, surprised. "Who knows what will happen next? Why are you asking it?"

"Because," murmured Sherry just above a whisper, "because—I should hate to think of you two quarreling. You're both rather proud and strong-willed."

"I won't take a step out of my way to antagonize him," he promised. "And I will accept his advice and experience wherever possible."

She sighed. "I couldn't ask any more of you. It seems silly to think you'd ever have reason to cross swords. It won't happen, mustn't happen. But—"

They were at the porch. Nickum stood in the doorway, calling down to them. "Well, I don't need to sleep on it, after all. We'll battle this business out. No matter who gets hurt, we're going to clean up the dirty stables from corner to corner. In the morning, Charterhouse, I want you to go to the Bowlus place with me. We start our campaign in that stretch of country and it's wise to show you around."

The girl murmured "good night" and turned in. Charterhouse saw her face white and troubled as she passed

the door; troubled and grieving over the bloodshed that
inevitably marched nearer, because she was a woman.
Nickum knocked the ashes from his pipe and silently followed her. Charterhouse swung along the porch to his
own room, entered and pushed the door nearly shut.
Through the small aperture remaining he watched the
yard with a close attention. A man slipped from another
dark angle and crossed quickly to the bunkhouses; instead
of going into any of them, he disappeared somewhere
beyond. A great deal later, when Charterhouse was in
bed, he heard spaced shots come faintly off the prairie.
His mouth tightened.

"There's a leak around here," he mused.

Meanwhile, Sherry Nickum stood in front of her mirror
and studied the dark reflection thrown back. In the course
of this eventful day she had discovered something that
both stirred and depressed her. A struggle as old as the
ages, yet as new as each life took hold of her heart. Until
it was settled she would never walk without one certain
picture in her mind—tall and exuberant Buck Manners
standing so indolently sure of himself in front of Clint
Charterhouse whose clean-chiseled features seemed wist-
fully pointed to the promise of happiness hiding beyond
the elusive horizons. She too heard the spaced shots; and
her eyes clouded.

Chapter SEVEN

"Consider Charterhouse to speak for me on any occasion when I am not personally with you," said old John Nickum, facing the assembled Box M riders. "When he gives an order, you are to obey it without qualification. Is that clearly understood? I want no doubts on the subject. This applies to everybody, no exceptions. From now on he is my right-hand man."

In the hot morning's sun he looked grim and gray; overnight he had aged. But the fighting flare was in the chilly eyes and the boom of his voice was as aggressive as ever. The group of men—Charterhouse counted forty in that crowd—stood silent. Haggerty shifted, no light relieving the sour, stringy face.

"I'm to work with him?" demanded the foreman, pitching the question in a surly tone.

Nickum stared down at the man long enough to make the silence oppressive. "I thought I made myself plain, Haggerty. You work under him, and no debate about it."

"I thought I was foreman of this outfit, Nickum."

"You still are—unless the job don't satisfy you. In that case—"

"I said nothing about not being satisfied," retorted Haggerty. "But it's a funny pass when a foreman don't run the spread direct under the owner. Charterhouse ain't friendly to me, and it goes hard on a man to take orders thataway."

Nickum turned to Charterhouse. "Want to declare yourself on that point?"

"Yes," said Clint. "Haggerty's got nothing to fear if he'll play poker with me. We had a run-in on the prairie and I took exception to some of his remarks. I still do.

But this is business, and I'll hold down my private opinions if he'll do the same."

"Hear that, Haggerty?" challenged Nickum.

"I heard," grumbled the foreman. "Agreeable to me."

"Now," went on Nickum, "I have got news for you boys. We are going to bust this country wide open. We're going to smash the outlaws if we have to wreck Casabella to do it. The gun's out. Anybody that happens to be a mite squeamish can bunch the job now. The rest of you will hold yourself ready to ride at any time, day or night. This morning Charterhouse and me are taking a little trip toward Angels. Haggerty, you pick ten men and cruise over toward Dead Man. Be back by noon. Look for anything interesting. Seastrom, you stick around the house and watch. Fitzgibbon."

A small, bald and oldish puncher with incredibly bowed legs inclined his head. "Yes, sir?"

"Take four-five riders and hit north and see how our stock lays up yonder. Also be back by noon. I want nobody ambling off alone from now on."

"You and Charterhouse are riding pretty light," observed Seastrom. "Ought to have somebody else along."

"Never mind," countered Nickum. "I've been shot at before. Come on, Charterhouse."

The two wheeled and trotted away from the home quarters side by side. All the prairie lay fresh before them. Dead Man's Range was clear on the east and the pine ridge stood up in the more immediate southwest, to which they were now going. For almost an hour they went racking along without a word, covering eight or nine miles and bringing the trees within a short hail. Nickum seemed plunged in unpleasant thoughts and Charterhouse had no desire to break in. For himself, he surrendered his senses to the clear, heady feel of the morning. Sun beating down warmly, the soft air pungent with earth's smell, and the vast distances reassuring him of the old, old freedom. It was a beautiful country; one he never wanted to leave. He brought himself out of a comfortable indolence to see Nickum dropping slightly behind. The old man appeared a little paler than usual.

"No hurry," grunted Nickum. "We'll take it easier. When a man rides the saddle forty years he gets some churned up inside. I'm about arrived at my rocking chair days, Charterhouse, and by gosh, I hate to think of it! I'd slice off all but ten acres of this range to be twenty years younger."

"That's why I cut loose and drifted," mused Charterhouse. "Wanted to kick up my heels before the sun went down."

"That's the way I was," replied Nickum with gruff regret. "Always wanted to feel my oats. Well, I got nothing to complain about. Lived a pretty full life. Came in here before the Indians left. Wild country and wild men. Even wilder than they are now. This present breed of rats can't teach me any tricks. I learned 'em all from tougher eggs than they ever will be. But I wish I was younger. Hell to want to be able to do things you can't any more. Ride forty miles, dance all night, and ride forty miles back to work all day. One time Buck Manners' dad and me hugged the lip of a water hole and fought a young army of rustlers ten straight hours." He checked his impulse toward reminiscence. "I brought you out here to show you some trails leading around Red Draw and through the pines. It's where we will do a lot of riding. Curly's hanging around Dead Man, but that don't fool me. He'll hook up with Shander's outfit and break for these pines. It's better shelter, closer to Box M and offers all of 'em a better chance to lick me. You've got to know where the best hiding places are."

"I overheard Shander and Curly speak of having thirty or thirty-five men in Dead Man."

Nickum was frowning at him. "Why didn't you spill that last night when Manners asked you?"

"We-ell," reflected Clint, hazel eyes narrowed against the increasing heat, "I sort of figured the information belonged to you privately. You're paying me, not Manners."

"Don't get any fool notions about him," emphasized Nickum. "That boy's straight as a string. I know that breed. Sorry you mistook his caliber. I'll tell him about that crew when I see him next. It's his right to know."

"You're the doctor," acquiesced Clint. "I thought I'd tell you first. Do what you want."

"So they figure to swamp me?" growled Nickum. "Well, I'll sprinkle some bait and bring that bunch right where I want. Should have cracked Curly in the head five years ago, before he got big ideas about himself. Now he's powerful and it'll take blood spilling. There's a lesson for you, Charterhouse. Never get tender-hearted over a crook. It only means a worse fight later on."

"Did you hear some shots beyond the ranch last night?" queried Charterhouse.

Nickum stared straight ahead for a matter of two or three minutes. "So you heard that, too? My boy, I made no mistake in picking you. I heard 'em. I know what it means. More than that, I've known I had some traitors in my outfit for a long time. That's what makes an old man out of me. Traitors on Box M and no way of catching on who they are. Damn that brand of a yellow belly!"

"Might be used to advantage," suggested Clint. "Let them get wind of your plans. They'll tattle. Then change your plans. For instance, the trail from Dead Man Range and from Shander's goes by Bowlus' place and through the trees into Angels. Let it be rumored you aim to station a few men there to pick off any hostile outfit that passes. Just say aloud you figure to put about a half dozen men in concealment."

"Then what?"

"Then send out your half dozen men and put them there."

"So Shander can swamp 'em, boy? He'll do that."

"Exactly," pursued Clint. "But at the last minute get about fifteen more men, take them on some wild goose chase so that there won't be any leak of information, and push them into your first bunch, then let Shander come."

Nickum grunted approval. "I don't see why I figured it necessary to show you around. But we'll hit down on Bowlus for a visit anyhow."

The country grew more seamy and undulating. They dipped and rose from one arroyo to another. A spur of the ridge reached out to meet them, but Nickum veered away to skirt the trees and keep in the open. Charterhouse swept the country with a more earnest attention; they passed stale tracks, stopped a moment to study them, and pressed on.

"Too many riders at night," muttered Nickum. "Sure sign of hell ready to bubble over. Turn a little more to the left. We're getting too close to those trees. I'd despise to die of a rifle shot."

"How big an outfit has this Manners got—and where is it?" questioned Clint.

"Northwest of me. His range runs about half as big as mine. Not so well watered and not so thrifty for stick, but—"

He was a few feet ahead of Charterhouse at the moment; in the middle of his sentence a shot cracked over the desert, breaking the sun-filled silence. Charterhouse instinctively spurred his horse around to cover the rancher on the ridge side. Nickum's face changed swiftly and he lifted his head in sudden pain toward the bright sky. Clint saw the old man's left hand reach down and press against his coat.

"The other way," panted Nickum. "He caught me from the prairie. In one of those arroyos—"

"Get down!" cried Charterhouse and crowded his horse against the rancher.

Another shot broke through the air; Charterhouse lifted Nickum bodily from the saddle and dropped him. Setting his spurs, he drove directly eastward, marking where a small dark spot stood against the rim of an arroyo a hundred yards away. As he flung himself forward he zigzagged his pony and lay flat against the horn, gun lifted. He caught the sun glinting on a rifle barrel. A distorted face lay along the butt of the gun, aiming carefully. Charterhouse yelled and fired, bringing up a scatter of dust. This caused the fellow to flinch slightly and his answering bullet went wild. Losing his cold killer's poise, he pumped the lead furiously and then rose erect and reached for his revolver, while Charterhouse swept down on him with a mad recklessness.

The ambusher began to step backward, once more

opening up. His lips moved and sweat poured across desperately frozen features; after one futile try he never pulled trigger again, for Charterhouse descended into the arroyo with dust rising thickly all around and plunged his lead across the point-blank interval. The ambusher coughed and sank, cursing. A choked cry for mercy came out of him; he rolled deeper into the arroyo and lay with his face pitched sightlessly to the sky.

Charterhouse reined about, staring at the dead man without pity. "Another dog dead," he muttered, hazel eyes flaring. "I've seen that mug before. At Shander's. They must have a gun artist hid in every damned prairie dog hole hereabouts." A horse stood away down the arroyo, indicating how far the ambusher had paralleled the riders before taking his chances. Charterhouse cantered on to the waiting animal, led it out of the arroyo and left it in plain sight for scouting riders to see. "Considering how shot with crookedness this country is, it won't be long before friendly pallbearers will be on the scene. Hardly before I turn my back, I reckon."

He returned swiftly to Nickum. The rancher had collapsed and lay on the sand, one elbow propping him up. Blood made a dull, irregular shield on his left side; all ruddiness was gone out of the old baron's face, and the steel-blue eyes held a glance that caused Charterhouse a stab of compassion.

"Get me on the horse ... and take me home," said Nickum, straining to get the words distinct.

"Bowlus' cabin is closer," Clint suggested tersely. He winced at the unspoken hint that Nickum would never live to see the end of that journey.

But the rancher insisted. "Get me on the horse. I'll die in my own bed. Won't leave my ghost in any other man's house. Hurry up, boy. I ain't immortal."

Clint hauled Nickum into the latter's saddle with considerable effort; the rancher seemed to have lost the use of his legs, but he gripped the horn with both big hands and steadied himself. Charterhouse mounted and closed in, offering one arm.

Nickum shook his head. "Make it under my own power. You get that fellow?"

"I got him."

"Circle thataway. Want to look at his face."

They went slowly to the arroyo and halted. Nickum looked down grimly. "Elva Smith—God pity the man. Used to work for me, then he went to the wild bunch. Let's go home."

They veered, established a true course to the northeast and settled down to a slow, tedious walk. The sun's heat increased and small atmospheric waves shimmered about them. Clint watched Nickum closely for the inevitable collapse and marveled that it was so long postponed. Nickum was dredging up the last dogged remnants of strength and making them serve his will.

"So Shander got me. Knew he would some day. Don't mind dying, but I wish I could last till sunset and feel the wind come. Always had a weakness for that time of day."

He shut his lips, conserving his strength; and not for an hour did he speak again. Then it was in close, small phrases. "Sherry's ranch. But you've got to stick and see it through. She'll marry Buck, but he ain't the right kind of a fighter. He's apt to go out and get his head blowed off, too. You won't. Too slick. I'll tell Sherry she's got to keep you till it's all done. Want you to sweep clean like a new broom. Promise that?"

"You've got it," muttered Clint.

"Good boy. We're almost home. I'll make it now."

Stubbornness alone brought him alive to the Box M quarters. Riders fanned out to meet them; Nickum waved all offers aside and drew up to his own house porch. Sherry ran out, crying suddenly. But Nickum, sliding into Clint's arms, gruffly rebuked her.

"No tears, girl. No tears, I don't—"

"Dad!"

"Hell, I can do anything once. Even die. Wait a minute, Charterhouse."

Clint stopped to let Nickum face the gathering crew. "Boys, it's Sherry's ranch now. I want you to mind her—and mind Charterhouse. Do what he tells you. He's going to fight it out. If you don't lick Casabella, I'll come back to haunt you, so help me."

Clint took him up the stairs and inside. Sherry opened a bedroom door and Clint put the old fighter down on the bed and stepped back.

"Home again," muttered Nickum, very pale. "Nice place to be. Sherry, you use your judgment in this matter. But give Charterhouse free rein to scrap it out the way he wants. I got a mighty big lot of faith in him. I reckon you'll marry Buck, but don't be in no hurry about it. Live a good long life and get as much fun out of it as I did. Well—"

Charterhouse turned and left the room. He knew the old man was dead before he got out of the door; Sherry had fallen beside the bed. Clint passed into the yard. It was beyond noon and Haggerty's party came racking in from their tour of inspection. A phrase ran out through the scattered hands.

"Nickum's dead."

Haggerty's sour face jerked up swiftly, darted all around and came to rest on Charterhouse. The latter saw a release of some tigerish emotion in the small, sullen eyes. Then the foreman got down and walked away.

"Mighty little sadness the news seems to cause him," reflected Charterhouse and returned to sit on the porch, waiting for Sherry to call him and meanwhile somberly thinking his way through the tangle of events.

The death of the old man had made a tremendous effect on the ranch. Charterhouse saw how moody and uncertain and dispirited the punchers in the yard were. They shifted about, collecting in knots, moving away, and collecting again. Old John Nickum's spirit had held them together and made a closely-welded, hard-riding clan out of them. Now they were lacking that inspiration and falling back to individual members, each doubting his own strength and perhaps fearing for his own safety. Box M was in danger of dissolution. Once that happened, the ranch was easy prey to marauding elements.

Yet anger and a desire for retribution were to be seen

also. The happy-go-lucky Seastrom reflected it by his rest-lessness, and others were likewise itching to be on the move. Out of this desire something might be done. But one thing was very certain—it would not do to let the crew go slack too long or they would lose morale. Charterhouse rolled a cigarette reflectively.

"Whoever runs the outlaw bunch is slick. He knew this very let-down would happen. He is planning on it. He means to use it for his big opportunity. Now, what would the man's first move be, and how soon would it be?"

That depended, he figured, on who ran the outlaw bunch. If Curly had the final word, then Curly would attack, being aggressive and impatient. Shander, on the other hand, was a trickier man, more subtle and might use nibbling tactics, like depleting Box M range, killing off individual Box M riders, breaking up the crew and starving out Sherry Nickum. Studd was ruthless and heavy-handed, but also had a eatlike caution and would move even more circumspectly. Not knowing what to expect, the wise policy would ordinarily have been to put things in order and wait out the renegades; considering the uneasy state of the crew's mind and the bushwhacking tactics so far employed, this was not possible. There was but one thing to do. Go out and attack. It didn't make much difference where. Anything to open up the outlaw ranks and provoke a general alignment of factions.

"Here I am talking like I owned this spread," he told himself. "Sherry might have different ideas. She might call everything off, sell the place or marry Manners. And that would certainly let me out. He wouldn't stand for my kind of fighting."

Seastrom and the grave, runty Fitzgibbon came over and squatted on the porch. Seastrom cleared his throat. "Who did it?"

"Nickum viewed the corpse and said it was a gent known as Elva Smith," replied Clint, conveying two pieces of information at once. He saw the men exchange a glance of tight satisfaction.

"You got him cold?"

"I got him."

"Two to your credit," grunted Seastrom. "No—three, including Graney. Seems to me you have done this outfit more good than the whole pack of us pitched together in the last two days. Elva Smith belonged to the wild bunch."

"A Shander man, too," put in Fitzgibbon who never had much to say.

Seastrom looked directly at Charterhouse. "We been talking things over with the rest of the bunch. It's general opinion that we'll string along behind you any time and place. The sooner the better and the rougher the better. That goes for all but about four boys who seem to have reservations on the subject. Naturally we ain't speaking for Haggerty. He'll have to announce himself."

"Which I guess he considers himself competent to do," replied Clint dryly. "I'm appreciating your trust in me, boys. If it was my spread, I'd move out now. But I won't say a word until I hear what Sherry's got to say—"

He broke off. Buck Manners, followed by four other riders came jauntily into the yard and drew up by the porch. The yellow-haired cattleman instantly caught the air of trouble.

"What's up?"

"Nickum in there—dead," muttered Seastrom.

Manners threw himself impetuously across the porch. "Sherry—Sherry, you poor kid." The door slammed behind him and Charterhouse heard the girl sobbing. He stared at his cigarette. "Sometimes sympathy is better kept down," he mused. "All he did was make her cry."

"If Manners takes over the place," observed Seastrom, "I dunno."

"I do," was Fitzgibbon's laconic interpection. "Palaver. More palaver. I'll quit."

The crying stopped. Man and girl were talking in there, his words running swiftly, hers very slow. Yet without attempting to eavesdrop, Clint thought her speech gathered strength as time went on. Presently the door opened and Manners nodded at Charterhouse with some impatience. Clint went inside, to find Sherry standing beside a chair, straight and white. She had fought back her weakness, meeting the grim necessities of the moment with supreme courage.. Her gray eyes touched Clint and remained on his face.

"I don't see why you have to bring Charterhouse into this," Manners was saying with the least trace of asperity. "It's between us, isn't it, Sherry?"

"I can't throw aside the directions my father left, Buck."

"I suppose not," countered Manners slowly and turned his attention to Clint. "I have told Sherry that the easiest way out is to let me take charge completely. Join the ranches. We might as well look at it frankly. We're to be married and it would have happened some day. Why not now? It would throw all this trouble on my shoulders and I doubt if there's any group of men in Casabella willing to tackle as big an outfit as mine and Box M put together. It seems a very simple and easy solution to me."

Sherry's eyes seemed to hold an appeal for Clint. He shook his head. "I reckon this is something I haven't got any part in, folks. It's your problem. I can say, however, that I'm ready to carry out what Sherry's dad intended me to do. If it is decided to fight the battle clear to the end, I'll do it."

"Why fight?" insisted Manners. "Double up the outfits under me and there won't be any fight. Shander and Curly can't muster enough men to beat me."

Rather reluctantly Clint found himself arguing against the idea, somehow feeling the girl wanted him to do so. "If that bunch of renegades have been willing to bust against Nickum, when they knew all along that you supported him, why wouldn't they be willing to bust against you alone? I don't see any difference. But it ain't my problem and I'll keep still."

"Thanks," was Manners short answer. Charterhouse caught the veiled antagonism and couldn't find it in his mind to blame the man. It was only human to resent the advice of an outsider. "Still," went on the yellow-haired ranchman, "I think it would take all the worry away from Sherry. Good Lord, she can't live here and go through a range war. Don't you understand, Sherry, that this is going to be mighty grim business? That pack of wolves might do anything. Anything, Sherry."

"I understand it better than you do, Buck" said the girl tonelessly. "Except for me, they have wiped out the family. I wouldn't even put it beyond them to kill me. What makes you think I don't understand war? Since I was old enough to know the meaning of words I have heard nothing but trouble and quarrel. Nothing but gun shots and hostility. I understand it so well, Buck, that I am going to go ahead just as my father wished. If I were like the ordinary woman, I'd call everything off. If I thought that peace would come for the asking, I would never let a Box M man lift a hand. But it won't—it never will. These beasts that creep in the night will never let us alone, until they are gone or we are gone."

"I think you ought to rely a little on my judgment, Sherry," pressed Manners. "It's a man's country."

"So it is," agreed the girl, "and I shall do as men do. Not because I want vengeance, but because until all that terrible crowd is wiped out there will be no end of sorrow. Clint, you go ahead. The ranch and all the men and all our resources are yours to use. Consider that you are in command. My father wanted it that way—and so it shall be. I am as much of a Nickum as he was."

Manners pressed his lips together. Once more Charterhouse got the impression of an enormous will and vitality surging in the man's body, ready to burst against barriers at any convenient opportunity. Manners was weighing him with the same calculation he had noticed in the saloon when they matched strength; the same flashing, fighting purpose glimmered in his blue eyes. Finally the ranchman shrugged his shoulders. "It amounts to turning me down, Sherry. Have I no place in your affairs at all? What makes you so sure Charterhouse is a better fighter than I am? It's yet to be proved."

"Be patient with me, Buck. And help us when Clint asks it. He has proved himself and you know it. I can't marry you until this is all settled. Then—"

"Then what?" insisted Manners, still struggling to keep the sharpness from his words.

The girl turned away. "We'll wait and see. Clint, will you send a man to Angels for a doctor?"

Clint nodded. Both men went out, leaving Sherry alone behind the closed door. Seastrom and Fitzgibbon waited on the porch, and Haggerty was crossing the yard slowly.

Manners rolled a cigarette, scowling at his finger tips. "Well, Charterhouse, it looks like you're first fiddle and I'm second. Seems you've done pretty well by yourself in the space of two days. Now what?"

Clint disregarded the latent antagonism. The waiting punchers drifted toward the porch. Haggerty slouched on the steps, staring at him without friendliness. "We're going to move out and start the ball. Right away."

"Can't you wait until Nickum's decently buried?" fretted Manners.

"I don't observe the other side standing on etiquette," replied Clint. "The question is, which way to hit. What would you do, Manners?"

"Wait them out," was the ranchman's prompt reply. "I believe in letting the other fellow lead from his chest."

"What would you do, Seastrom?"

"I'd hightail into Dead Man Range and bust up Curly," opined the puncher.

"Too much chasing around," countered Clint. "He'd play hide and seek with us until our tongues were hanging out."

"Right," agreed Fitzgibbon. "Why play another gent's favorite game? Better idea is to swarm down on Shander's joint and burn it to the ground and take that buzzard out to the nearest tree."

"You fellows are talking too much lynch law," stated Manners abruptly. "I said I'd stand behind you, Charterhouse, and I mean it. But I won't be a party to unprovoked attack. Whatever we think of Shander or the others, at least we ought to have some open act of aggression on their part before we take so much authority in our hands. You've got to abide by some rules."

Charterhouse began to see why old John Nickum had doubted his prospective son-in-law's ability in rough and tumbling fighting. Manners kept singing the song of order-

© Lorillard 1974

King Size
or Deluxe 100's.

KENT

WITH
THE FAMOUS MICRONITE FILTER

DELUXE LENGTH

DELUXE LENGTH KENT

you have
taste for quality,
ou'll like the taste
f Kent.

Kings: 16 mg. "tar," 1.0 mg. nicotine;
100's: 18 mg. "tar," 1.2 mg. nicotine
av. per cigarette, FTC Report Mar. '74.

© Lorillard 1

KENT
MENTHOL
WITH
The FAMOUS MICRONITE FILTER

DELUXE LENGTH

KENT MENTHOL

Try the crisp, clean taste of Kent Menthol 100's.
The only Menthol with the famous Micronite filter.

Menthol: 18 mg. "tar," 1.2
mg. nicotine; av. per cigarette,
FTC Report Mar. '74.

liness while the lawless elements in Casabella laughed. Some curious streak of hesitancy seemed to blend in with the ranchman's otherwise frank and rowdy nature.

Clint turned to Haggerty. "What's your opinion?"

But Haggerty sourly rejected the invitation. "I'll listen to wise men. You're supposed to do the thinking, ain't you?"

"Correct," assented Charterhouse, refusing to rise to the bait. "Sherry Nickum has told me to go ahead and fight my own style. I'm sorry to say I can't see Manners' desire to walk humbly. There can be no doubt about Shander or Curly, none whatsoever. They made their bed and they know what to expect. We'll never get any place by waiting for somebody else to be shot. From today on there will be nothing but straight, stiff fighting, and if anybody in this crowd doesn't like the looks of it, or if anybody doesn't feel he wants to take my orders and do as he's told, then I want him to speak up now, get his war bag and quit."

Absolute silence met the challenge. Clint waited a little while and went on, feeling he had the crew with him. "I'm not always going to take the trouble to explain things as we go. When we ride, we ride fast. When we hit, we hit hard. Seastrom, I want you to take eight men, pack a little cold grub in your roll, and hit down the trail toward Angels. Make camp in the trees below the Bowlus place where the road from Dead Man cuts over the ridge to town. Keep out of sight. Curly's outfit and Shander's uses that trail a lot. Take whatever comes along."

Seastrom rose with a suppressed grin. "That sounds good to me," he stated. Manners shook his head.

"Not to me. It's a style of war I don't approve of. I'll lend a hand against any attack they make, but I won't send men bushwhacking, Charterhouse."

"Won't ask it," delcared Charterhouse. "But will you send one of your men for the doctor? I can't trust a single Box M man in Angels."

"I'm riding down there on a quick trip. I'll see to it." Manners swung to the saddle and gathered his riders. He studied the Box M crew thoughtfully. "You boys are hell-bent on fighting now. But when some of you get riddled, you'll see my policy is better. However, I'm not the boss. Whatever happens, I'll be keeping a watch on the ranch-house. There'll always be one of my men cruising around to see that nothing happens to Sherry. I'll hold you personally to account if anything does happen to her, Charterhouse. I'll be back tonight to take care of old John's funeral."

Clint nooded and watched the group swing south. Seastrom had gone about his chore enthusiastically and was even now bringing up his chosen riders. One of them went to the kitchen for cold grub.

Clint beckoned Seastrom apart from the rest and spoke a low warning. "Watch your flanks, Heck. Don't be taken by surprise."

Seastrom looked lazily at him. "I was wondering if you had some other reason for sending us down there."

"Sugar draws flies," said Clint. "Do what I tell you—and don't move away from that trail until you get word."

Seastrom winked blandly. "I guess you're dry behind the ears." He motioned his party to follow. They filed past the kitchen, got their provisions and posted along in pursuit of Manners' party.

Charterhouse turned back and spoke to Fitzgibbon. "You collect ten more hands, Fitz. We're riding another way. May not be back tonight. Now the rest of you," nodding at the assembled crew, "are to stick tight. Keep a strict watch and let nobody surprise you. Haggerty, you're in charge of quarters. Keep a guard out tonight. You've got about fifteen men and that's ample to stave off any sort of trouble."

"I reckon I know my business," grunted Haggerty.

So far Charterhouse had let the foreman's hostile talk pass unnoticed. He saw now it was time for him to challenge Haggerty so that the crew would know exactly where he stood.

"Listen, if I didn't think you knew your business, you'd be on your way. You work with me—or you take your time and walk. Is that clear?"

"I'm a Box M man," growled Haggerty. "And was one long before you came. I know what to do. I'll stick. But that ain't saying you and me won't settle our private argument some of these days."

"I'm looking forward to the time—with interest," drawled Charterhouse.

Haggerty glared harshly at him and stalked away. Fitzgibbon was organizing the second group of riders as quickly and efficiently as Seastrom had the first, but with only a tenth of the talk and energy. The more Charterhouse saw of this quiet, unromantic little man the better he liked him. Haggerty had stopped by the barn and was talking to one of the men covertly; Clint paid a moment's attention and then went into the house and shut the door.

Sherry Nickum sat in a chair, looking at him with queerly set features. It seemed to Clint she had fought so hard to suppress the grief and tragic remembrance that the struggle had left her bereft of strength. Even so, his throat tightened from the effect of her slim, relaxed beauty, and he had difficulty in carrying out his calm announcement.

"I'm moving," said he. "Don't know when I'll be back, nor do I know what will happen. But we're riding, and it seems likely we'll lock horns with the renegades somewhere along the line. Maybe it appears as if we're hurrying the business unduly. For me, I see nothing but danger in further delay."

She rose from the chair and came to him, gray eyes blurring. "I want you to do what you think best. I'll hold up my part—"

Then she gave way at last, swaying against him, a wild burst of emotion beating against his chest. Like a father, he put his arms around her while the minutes went by and her body trembled to the torrent so suddenly released. Then the sound of her crying died in the quiet room and her voice came up, muffled and small.

"Sorry, but I had to get it out of me, Clint. I'm through now and the worst of the hurt is over. Take care of yourself. Be as kind and just as you can in this terrible business. That's all I can say. I've lived in Casabella too long ever to expect a happy ending. Always it has been black curses, killings, treachery and brutality. I will stay here, no matter what happens. And . . . be careful."

She drew away, and as he turned he caught one glimpse of her white, clear face. Then he was on the porch, finding his party ready. He mounted and led it nòrth along the yard, halting once to give Haggerty a last order. "Get the handy man to turn out a box for Nickum—and the rest of it. Don't leave this place until you hear from me."

"Where'll you be?" challenged Haggerty, a glint of slyness in the sullen eyes.

"Somewhere north of here," replied Clint, and pressed on. He swept on out into the prairie. Some time after he looked back and discovered a rider cutting away from the ranch to the southwest; and he smiled grimly.

Chapter EIGHT

Blind Bowlus sat on his doorstep that evening and stirred uneasily the crisp air. During the late afternoon his sharp ears had picked up the tremble of riders going rapidly southward through the pines. The average man would have missed the sound but Bowlus, almost sightless, absorbed the news of the world through his ears with an ability approaching the miraculous. The average man, also, would have thought nothing about these casual rumors of hoofbeats. Here again Bowlus knew better. The very tempo of the air first interested, then warned him. Later he heard the brush crackling back of his place, dying so suddenly that he knew an ambush had been established. At dusk a single rider had passed completely around the clearing on a scout, whereupon Bowlus grunted scornfully, "Damn fool, I couldn't draw a bead on him, blind as I be. Nobody fools old Bowlus."

All this was preliminary. He ate his supper, full in the knowledge that this little clearing was the center around which forces groped and parried for advantage. Dusk passed into dark and for a short interval the world was in the spell of a deep, pervading stillness. Bowlus, true to his habits, smoked a pipe, cheeks slightly turned to catch the first faint runner of night's breeze. He loved to rest on the stoop and feel the universe absorb the dying day, to wait for the first sound of wind in the leaves and to catch, through the blurred windows of his soul, the first faint sparkle of stars. These were elementary pleasures, but all that Bowlus had left to him; and like some pagan he steeped himself in the peace and vast serenity of it. Yet not this evening; his sensitive mind was alive to the impalpable threats of forthcoming struggle, his solitude destroyed. And because he was part and parcel of the rangeland he clenched his old fists and shook them outward.

"If I had my sight back—just for a month, even—they could cut me down and be damned to 'em. I'd ride with Box M again, I would. I'd swallow smoke and sling lead and sweat blood, like they're sure going to do. Just one more lick, that's all I'd ask. Hell, better be dead than useless."

He drew in his arms and listened. A stray fragment of sound came slow and soft over the clearing. His dog, crouched by the steps, rose and stiffened. Bowlus said, "Shut up, Tige," and ran a hand over the beast to discover which way he pointed. The dog's muzzle was against the east, trembling with a suppressed growl. "You hush, Tige, and mind your own business." A bit of metal jingled. Then all this faded and was lost for a full five minutes. Bowlus grew rigid, teeth clamping around the stem of his pipe. Fear came to him, the first time in years of lonely living. For the first time he felt a physical presence threatening his own safety. Somebody stood near by, ominously silent. Bowlus gripped the dog at his side with swift pressure to keep the animal from baying; instinctively he felt that his own life depended on remaining still and seemingly ignorant. So he talked idly to the dog.

"Fine evening. Fine, large evening, Tige. Stars is awful big tonight. Been a sort of a hot day, but she's a nice breeze right now. Yessir, Tige, we got a good quiet place to live."

Tige resisted his pressure and broke into a vicious growl. A voice near by muttered, "Keep that brute quiet or I'll strangle him, Bowlus."

Bowlus relaxed at the sound of the voice. The sinister silence was broken, his senses made contact with reality. Moreover, he knew the fellow. Out of the vast gallery of tones he had catalogued and stored away he took the rather high-pitched, immature voice of Curly and matched it with the present talk. It fitted.

"Lord sakes," he muttered, "you scared me." And for diplomatic reasons he went artlessly on. "Kind of upsets a blind gent like me to be disturbed by a stranger after dark."

"Don't know who I am, uh?"

"I can scarcely see daylight, let alone a face in the dark."

Curly advanced. Bowlus saw the flicker of a hand passing in front of his eyes, but kept his head very still. "I always wondered just how blind you was," grumbled Curly. "I seen too many tricks in my life to be took to camp. But I reckon you're really sightless."

"Blind as a bat. I reckon you might be hungry. Most riders coming my way are. Step in and I'll toss a can o' beans for you—"

Curly interrupted. "Anybody around here, old man?"

"Just me and my dog."

Curly whistled softly. In another moment Bowlus made out riders sifting through the trees. Curly had edged into the cabin for a look. He came out again and walked off, softly giving orders to somebody. Then he returned and laid a hand on Bowlus' shoulder, pressing down hard. "You tell me the truth, old buzzard, or I'll take pleasure in laying my gun across that brittle skull of yours. I'd do it, too, savvy? Nobody around these woods, uh?"

"It's been awful quite today," said old Bowlus. "I ain't talked to a soul."

"Hear anything? Don't lie!"

Bowlus, from the tone of the outlaw's voice, visualized Curly leaning forward wolfishly, half-inclined to strike. So he decided on half-truth and spoke softly. "I think a spread o'men passed along the trail a spell before dark."

"Which way?"

"Towards Angels."

"Heard anything since—any brush rattle, any gear squeak, horses, or like that? Has your dog been uneasy. Smell anything in the wind?"

"Not till you come," said Bowlus. "But—" and he affected sudden mystery, "that bunch didn't seem to come back from Angels."

A long silence. Men were moving with sibilant swiftness about the clearing. Curly had gone off once more and Bowlus thought he was rid of the man. But the renegade was like a cat, evading even Bowlus' preternaturally sharp ears; without warning he was back, grumbling, "I don't trust you, not for a minute. When I see a stray horse on the landscape, I want to kill him or put him in my string. Same applies to you. Maybe you're a harmless duffer, but on the other hand you might be bait. Don't say anything, don't move outside of your cabin tonight. I'm watching this place all the time. If I—"

Bowlus waited patiently. He felt them ease off into the woods and it appeared as if the meadow was free of their presence again. His dog alternately lay stiffly silent or rose to growl. Somewhere in the high ground he caught the snap of a bough.

"Trap," he decided. "But who set it, Box M or Curly? Looks to me as if Box M had done such, for Curly acted like he smelled a rat. What brought him over? This ain't his country. I'd like to know what them shots meant this morning."

The breeze grew sharper; the man's old bones protested the cramped position he had so long held. Rising, he pushed the dog inside the house and followed, closing the door. Match in hand, he forebore striking it. A light would only bring grief on his head. Better to wait in the cold. Sit and wait, for sleep was not to be this blood-scented night.

"Tige, if I only had sight—"

Then he drew a great sigh and leaned against the wall. A single shot sent up a muffled echo amid the trees above the clearing. After this was a short lull, a breathless suspense as if the creatures of the earth were cringing away from man's sinister folly. It was only a moment. Another shot sounded, waking somewhere a swift reply. A ragged fusillade developed to the west of the cabin, sagged in strength and threatened to die out. The parties yonder were sparring for advantage, uncertain of each other's location and strength, shifting rapidly, swinging about the fringe of the meadow. A lone rider raced down from the ridge and cut in front of the cabin, slinging a bullet into the door as he passed. Bowlus heard the smack of the slug in the wall and deliberately sat down on the floor.

"Tige, you come here. Lay behind me. That's right—lay flat."

Curly seemed to have found a point of attack, for the gunplay strengthened wickedly farther southward where the Angels Dead Man trail came up from the desert. No longer was the firing sporadic or aimless. Detonations ran into each other wickedly like corn popping; one wild halloo floated back to the meadow. Bowlus listened eagerly. "Must be twenty-thirty men in that play," he reflected. "Don't appear to me as if the trap worked."

His attention swung to the north side of the meadow, picking up the drive of another outfit galloping recklessly through the trees. Presently they were in the meadow, flashing by the house single file, a long line of them with leather squealing and a single voice rising above the noise of advance. "Swing out and come abreast. Fitz, you haul over and hold the right end of our front. West more—and come on!"

"Charterhouse," grunted Bowlus. "I knowed he had a good character first time I heard him talk. Now, Curly, you damn hound! Sit still, Tige, I ain't talking to you."

Bowlus was too thoroughly a Box M man to stay silent any longer, so he got up and went to the door. There was a touch of powder smell in the breeze that called him to battle and he gripped the casing with his gnarled fingers, swearing bitterly. Charterhouse's party was temporarily absorbed in this mystery. But within a minute or two Bowlus caught the swelling echoes as they pitched back to him. The fight became more grimly intense, more voices rose, and the doubling fury of the fire weltered through the trees. They had ceased moving and were in a stand-to conflict. So much he could determine by the steady spat and crack reverberating from the same location. Like men rooted in one spot and jolting each other with blind anger. Sooner or later somebody had to give way; energy and bullets lasted only about so long. Bowlus' practised ears detected a faltering presently and another shifting. Part of the echoes came from a more remote angle of the trees, guns blasted away from wider vantage points. The engagements turned fitful, firing died. A pair of horsemen raced

toward the cabin, wheeled around it. Bowlus dropped to
the earth as they thundered by. Lead passed over him,
shattering his window. He heard them breathing hard,
heard them muttering back imprecations, heard them
fleeing east into the open prairie.

"Curly's men," exulted Bowlus. "They took a hiding,
by gosh!"

Bowlus started to rise, then scuttled to another side of
the cabin and flattened in the deeper darkness. A whole
party swept back from the south, turned into the clearing
and halted. Scouts broke away, searching around.

Charterhouse's voice called anxiously. "Bowlus."

Bowlus rose and felt his way back to the front. "Give
'em a drubbing, did you?"

He heard a mutter of relief. More men were coming
from the scene of battle. Somebody coughed. Bowlus recognized the cause of it with pity. He also picked up Heck
Seastrom's usually easy-going tones cold with rage. "The
buzzards will pay this bill in full before we get through,
boys. Take Lee in and put him on Bowlus' bunk. As for
Pink, ain't no use. He's done."

"Bowlus, I'm relieved to see you. Curly make any
threats?"

"Yeah, but nothing else. You whipped him?"

"Not enough, Bowlus. Not near enough. Anybody ride
back this way?"

"Couple gents fogging for the open hell-bent. But the
meadow's empty."

Charterhouse seemed to be holding a conference with
the others. "Think Curly held his bunch pretty well together. They've all gone west, which means Angels, I
guess."

"Mebbe we ought to have followed," suggested Seastrom.

"No advantage," decided Charterhouse. "The idea in
this was to keep the percentage on our side. Never play
their game. Surprise 'em. I think we crippled four-five,
but that ain't fair enough exchange for one man dead and
one man hurt."

"Then what?" asked Seastrom.

"I'd like to know what they figure to do next," mused Charterhouse. "If Curly goes to Angels, the rest of the pack will be there soon enough. Well, I think I'll drift in by myself and see if I can pick up any dope."

"Not wise," said Fitzgibbon.

"Take me," put in Seastrom.

"No, I'll creep in alone. You boys stay right here until I come back. Meanwhile, somebody will have to ride to Box M and see if the doctor is there. Bring him back for Lee. As for Pink, I hate to say it, but he'd better be buried here and now. We may move fast before daylight."

"Why not cut for Shander's and clean out the joint since we know Curly ain't reinforcing him at present?"

"Move like that would be liable to place us beyond a quick run to Box M. Above all, boys, we've got to keep tab on these Curly wolves. That reminds me, a man had better go up and camp on the ridge trail to see nobody slides up during the dark. Same for the Dead Man trail. We've got our finger on Curly and we can't let him ease off to unknown directions. I'm going. Stick tight. This is a game of checkers. Party that does the most jumping wins. Our idea is to keep the other bunch out of our king row."

"Take Seastrom," said Fitzgibbon. "Two's better'n one. You'll hear more and see more."

"All right. Let's ride, Heck."

"If you ain't back by daylight," went on Fitzgibbon with unusual loquacity, "I'll bust into Angels."

"We'll be back before midnight," promised Clint, swinging away.

"Ain't sure," grumbled Fitzgibbon. "That town is the original breeding place of sin and treachery."

The two left the meadow and tracked over the scene of fighting. Shortly beyond they took the more open area to the west. But once timber began to rank around them Charterhouse led off and hit independently into the ridge. So, silently, they passed across it and lined out for Angels, the lights of which beckoned sardonically at them through the distance. The wind was fresh and clear, the night very dark. From afar one lonely shot faintly reverberated.

"Angels celebrating in its homely, hospitable manner," grunted Seastrom, breaking the long silence.

Charterhouse had been thinking of Casabella politics. "Listen, Heck. We'll say Curly fights because he's a born herd jumper. We'll say Studd plays the same game because he is a sort of peanut politician and looking out for himself. We'll go so far as to admit Wolfert is doing what he is told to do. But Shander—what does he stand to gain by tipping over the bucket? He's got land and cattle. If he loses this ruction, he also loses his property. I don't quite get it. Ain't natural to play so hard for a plumb uncertain stake."

"Casabella style, Casabella fever."

"Always some sort of reason for fevers," countered Clint. "It appears to me there must be a nigger in the woodpile we've overlooked."

Seastrom's reply was slow and cautious. "Any names to add to the list?"

"None. But I believe there's some motives, at present unknown, to add to the list."

"Mebbe, but what of it? We've got plenty of motives to start all the needful friction. We'd better turn off to hit Angels behind the slaughterhouse. It's deserted. Easy place to leave the horses."

Accordingly they veered and slid off from the town's front side. A quarter hour of slow travel brought them near the slaughterhouse. Dismounting, they went forward, Seastrom leading. The windmill was turning and the joints squeaked badly; water trickled in the gloom. Seastrom kept swerving one way and another until he stopped Charterhouse in the lee of a stinking shed.

"Safe enough here," he whispered. "What next?"

"You keep to this side of town, Heck. Cruise along back with your eyes and ears open. I'm cutting around the plaza. Want to see if Shander's in town. We may get some ideas out of the trip. Don't take any chances. Meet me here in about an hour."

"Listen, I ain't so strong for splitting up. This is one tough joint."

"I know, but we'll stand a better chance of getting information that way. But if I don't show up in time, you wait an extra hour and pull out alone. That's to keep Fitz from becoming too nervous. He ain't to move away from the clearing until I get back."

"You're the doctor," assented Seastrom.

They walked the length of the slaughterhouse and reached the back of a store building. Seastrom halted. Charterhouse murmured, "Take it easy," and slipped off. He paused at a narrow alley and saw a small section of the dark plaza down the far end; men crossed his vision and vanished. There was the sudden lure to follow the alley and come out among them, but he disregarded it and went on, studying a beam of light that came through a back door and lay directly across his path. He hesitated, heard voices, and shot over the revealing rays on the run to find himself at the stable's rear. Familiar territory.

Peering down the length of the interior, Clint discovered sundry citizens of Angels leisurely loitering under a lantern suspended from the rafters. A gust of laughter came to him, and he put aside temptation for the second time, pressing around a corral and reaching the open desert. Soundlessly he faded into it.

He had only that moment disappeared when a man flung open the same back door he had recently skirted and ran forward as far as the stable. The man crouched in the darkness, staring all about the shadows of the corral; then he rose and ran beyond the stable and swept the cloaked prairie carefully. A grunt of dissatisfaction escaped him. Doubling back, he went down the stable's vault, out the front and across the plaza hurriedly. About the same time a rider came loping into Angels from eastward and hauled his pony to a cruel stop by Studd's saloon. Dismounting, he thrust a surly question at one of the bystanders. "Where's Wolfert?" The bystander nodded his head, and the rider tramped beyond the saloon a few buildings into a door.

Clint Charterhouse, flat on his belly at the plaza's southwest corner, saw the rider go in. It was too dark to determine the fellow's identity but there was a familiar carriage about those shoulders that interested him. Silently he considered the proposition. "Looks like he was in a hurry. Good news or bad news, maybe, which he wants to impart. Who'd he impart it to if not the wise gents in charge of this scrap? That means he's gone in yonder door to find them. Proceeding from which—"

He got up and slid into the shadows, fouled himself in baling wire and scented the proximity of stale beer kegs. He was behind Studd's, hearing the swell of talk that emerged. A second-story window lifted to considerable profanity and an empty bottle fell beside him. Farther on he began to listen for particular voices. The building next to Studd's seemed empty and adjacent to that was a store. Beyond the store ran a shorter tenement containing a back porch. He settled on the porch and put his eye to a keyhole, discovering only darkness.

"Let's consider," he muttered. "The fellow went one, two, three doors from Studd's. This must be it. No lights, no sound. I wonder if there's a room between me and the front end—and what am I getting into?"

He stepped away from the porch, scanning the upper windows. "Grated, which means jail above and sheriff or marshal's office below. Now—"

Unexpectedly he discovered men poking along the back of town. A boot slammed into a box near the saloon and somebody's surly curse rolled sluggishly through the darkness. At almost the same time another questing citizen moved up from the opposite buildings, speaking with impatience. "Why don't you sound the fire bell and let everyone know where you are? For the love o' gosh, be quiet about it. Tim, see anything?"

"No, and it's a fool business."

"Well, he's skulking around these premises somewhere. Come this way. We'll drag along every building."

Several men came toward Clint Charterhouse, pinching him in from both sides. He was trapped in the small area. Crawling over the porch, he tested the knob of the back jail door; it gave to pressure and emitted the smell of musty leather and burlap sacks. More important, it also gave him the rumble of talk from some front room of the place. Momentarily the searchers approached. He even saw their dim outlines swaying forward.

"Try that jail yard. I'm telling you he's around somewhere. But don't wake the dead. We want to catch him off balance."

"Who is it?"

"Charterhouse, who'd you suppose? Didn't Haggerty—"

Clint slid inside the room and softly closed the door against them. A shaft of light seeped below an inner portal, along with the aroma of tobacco smoke. A chair scraped. Immediately he recognized the sullen, surly tones of the Box M foreman. Haggerty himself!

"I'm taking a big chance in coming away from the ranch. It might mean my hide."

"You was sent, wasn't you? That's a fair excuse."

"Yeah, I was sent down to warn the bunch at Bowlus' place. But I ought to've hit right back instead of dallying into Angels. Seastrom and Charterhouse are both here. Fitz told me they was. Said Charterhouse had given orders for the bunch to stay put until they scouted this joint."

Studd's unmistakable rumble came through. "I call that gall. Seastrom's crazy enough to put his head in a trap, but this Charterhouse is a cool, hard number. I'm thinking we got a man to deal with as stiff as old John was himself. And the gal gave Charterhouse a free hand?"

"Absolutely," growled Haggerty.

"I'd sure like to know how Mister Buck Manners takes that," said Studd ironically. "Him expecting to marry Sherry Nickum and still nosed out by a total stranger. Hell, that's rich."

Charterhouse stood in the middle of the black little room, mind devouring every scrap of phrase that came to him. Haggerty was a traitor, yet the news somehow failed to surprise him much. His estimate of the man's character had not been high in the first place and this new revelation only bore out the judgment he had formed. But what did Haggerty mean in saying he had come from Box M to warn the men at the Bowlus place? Listening intently, Clint was disturbed by the nearing sounds of the search party outside. They were going around the area with a fine-tooth comb.

"It don't make things no easier for us," put in Haggerty.

"Nor harder," was Studd's reply. "If they start scrapping among themselves, for control of Box M, we get all the breaks."

The almost girlish voice of Curly cut in. "Quit shaking hands with yourself, Studd. I lost men tonight and I don't propose to sit around and grin about it. Get busy and give us some ideas."

"I ain't running this show, Curly."

"Well, by gosh, if somebody don't take a heavier hand in the situation, I'll crack Box M wide open. I been wanting to do it a long while. What's the use of fiddling? Everybody knows what we're trying to do anyhow. Why beat about the bush? Sock 'em hard and get it done. There ain't anybody in Casabella able to stop us."

"We had ought to be out looking for those two buzzards right now," stated Haggerty.

"The longer they stick here the more they hang themselves," said the unexcitable Studd. "You boys never have learned to play a patient game."

"Too much patience all around—"

Somebody came into the office. Studd spoke with a slightly more suave manner. "We had to send for you, Shander. Things is sort of moving to a point."

Curly interrupted, explaining the fight and its consequences. Shander stopped him. "I have already heard about it. Heard about the whole business. Know just where everybody is now."

"Well, then," snapped Curly, "do something, or I'll make a play of my own and pull out."

"What would that be?" demanded Shander coldly.

There was a short silence. Curly started speaking in a slightly lower tone. Charterhouse heard the beginning, "My idea is to use—" and the rest of it was erased by a more immediate distraction. The searchers back of the buildings were stubbornly returning to their first scent. They began to advance on the jail.

"He come 'round this way," said someone. "And he ain't had no chance to slip off." Boots crossed the porch, a hand fell on the doorknob. "He's hiding close by. You wait, I'm going through and see Studd." The door opened slowly as Charterhouse backed into a corner and slipped his gun free. Another moment and the man stood within five feet of him, breath rising and falling; and in still another breath he would be across, opening the inner portal and throwing a revealing ray upon the back room. Certain exposure. Rigid, mind flashing around to find a loophole of escape, Charterhouse heard Shander say, "Well, that's a good idea, Curly, and the one I came to offer myself. We'll act on it. Tomorrow. Fort Carson. Keep your men—"

The searcher crossed the room, stumbled over a discarded saddle and groped for the inner knob. Charterhouse raised his gun, suddenly cold and nerveless. He was trapped before and behind.

Chapter NINE

During the first half hour Seastrom had considerable stealthy excitement to stir his reckless blood. Knowing the town perfectly, he ranged behind the buildings with considerable confidence. Madame LeSeur's hotel was the last along the line; the kitchen door stood wide open and the dishwasher, a frowsy and rheumatic graduate of Box M, slammed cups and plates around his sink with tired petulance. The savor of cooked food actually brought pain to hungry Heck Seastrom's jaw hinges. From his covert position he saw a table six feet away on which stood leftovers from supper; a few cooked steaks, a bowl of potatoes, a platter of cabbage, and all the accessory garnishments. The thought of this food for Madame's crowd rankled, aroused his sense of injustice; and when so moved, Seastrom was of a nature that acted on impulse. Save for the dishwasher, who was more or less bound by the fraternal ties of the old ranch, the kitchen was empty. Seastrom looked into the darkness, skipped nimbly over the doorsill and had two robust, though stiffly cold steaks in his fist when the dishwasher turned. Being a tired and feeble man, he grunted mildly. Seastrom was back in the shadows before the former finally spoke.

"Ain't a safe place for you, Heck."

Seastrom chuckled. "I wish you'd keep my meat warm." He ate with subdued violence. "You ain't seen me, Pot. So forget it."

"I ain't seen you, but somebody will," said the sudsy Pot. "It's a damn tight town. Now sift before that wall-eyed cook—"

This designated personage entered from the dining room at the moment, a very obese fellow with pouched

114

eyes and an unfavorable attitude. "Who you talking to, Pot?"

"Reciting Shakespeare to m'self," grunted the dishwasher.

The cook eyed the meat platter and detected the slimmer contents. "This Shakespeare another bum wanting a handout, huh? I told you plenty time to give no grub free." And the cook made for the door. Seastrom had stripped one T-bone down to an almost polished surface. Backing off into deeper protection, he took careful aim with it and threw. The bone struck the cook so hard that the gentleman's stomach reverberated like a drum. Seastrom chuckled and effected a falsetto voice. "Sorry I can't stay to chop wood, you inflated left-hand cousin to a weasel. So long." He ran down the line of buildings, paused to finish the other T-bone and to get his bearings. He felt better, he felt vigorously inclined.

An alley yawned upon him and he went along it until he stood indiscreetly beside a party of Curly's riders who had just come from the dining room. Their talk interested him, since it was the other side's version of the recent fight. But he gleaned nothing of importance and his sober judgment made him retreat. So after scanning the plaza and noting the rather large number of horses at the racks, he went back and continued his prowl. At the stable he again risked his skin and cat-walked down the vault. Men were just strolling away, crossing to Studd's. Evidently the roustabout had gone with them, for nobody seemed to be left behind, and after reassuring himself of the fact, Seastrom deliberately lounged to the sidewalk and draped himself against a wall.

"Loaded for bear," he told himself, scanning the town. "Must be thirty or forty riders here. You don't draw that many men together without it meaning some sort of hell."

Another party of about ten men racked in and halted at Studd's. Seastrom saw Shander in the saloon light and he pursed his lips thoughtfully. Shander was top dog of all this business, the king pin. His presence meant action; he was the jasper who gave orders. "They had that fight framed. Got word of us being around the Bowlus place plenty soon, all right. Now who spilled the beans? Shander's come to get the score on that affair, and I hope it chokes him. I wish I heard what his orders were."

That reminded him of Charterhouse. He began to worry. The designated hour was nearly gone, and the feeling of Angels was beginning to touch Heck Seastrom's nerves. There was such a thing as overstaying a visit. Some fool might stumble upon the horses and raise an alarm, upon which Angels' gates would be soon shut.

Contemplating the plaza through narrowed lids, Heck detected a tremor of excitement near the saloon. Five or six men broke away and hurried off, skirting the town's southwestern corner, like terriers smelling game. Another fellow cut straight across the plaza, and bore down on the stable. Seastrom calculated his chances in the grateful gloom and decided to stay put. The fellow passed him, plunging on through the driveway, and Seastrom, taut-muscled, identified Sheriff Wolfert. "Going so fast his shirt tail's flapping," muttered the dynamic puncher. Instantly was born a rash decision. He let Wolfert get out in the back area before trotting silently in pursuit.

The sheriff had swung along the back line in the direction of Madame LeSeur's. "Wonder if that drum-bellied cook told him? Well—" He followed carefully. Wolfert stopped. A door opened and the sheriff ducked inside. Seastrom approached, drawing himself more tightly to the building wall at each step; he had not reached nearer than twenty feet of the door when Wolfert came out, illumined in a patch of light, and started back.

Coming so rapidly, Seastrom was caught unprepared. Instantly he obeyed his fundamental instinct, which was to use his own magnificent strength. Throwing out both arms, he smashed into the fast-traveling Wolfert and snapped all his muscles into a mighty bone-crushing hug. The impact carried both of them to the ground, Wolfert, unloosing a strangled yell and twisting as some madman.

"Here, cut that out!" grunted Seastrom. "You want the whole town to know what's going on? Oh, so you do, do you! Well, if I got to smack you—"

Somebody ran out of the hotel kitchen and Seastrom found himself trapped. That yell had wakened the town; there was a sudden traffic around the stable. Lights popped out of second-story windows. Seastrom, unable to control Wolfert's knees and finding the resistance more than he had calculated, decided to wind up a bad bargain before he was swamped. Letting go with one-hand, he started to rise. Wolfert pulled him back to the ground, shouting again. The hotel cook responded. "I'm coming. Hold on—"

"Hold hell!" grunted Seastrom, going hog-wild. He cramped the sheriff in his arms, hoisted the man bodily, whirled and flung him into the cook's path with every cataclysmic ounce of strength. He heard the impact and it satisfied him. Without further argument, he leaped away from the buildings, setting a dead course for the slaughterhouse. Then the shooting began. The cook yelled frantically. Wolfert lifted a gasping warning. Bullets clipped along the earth to either side of Seastrom but he refused to open a return fire and reveal his location. Diving around the slaughterhouse, he straightened in a mad rush, reached the stinking hide shed and seized his horse.

"Now I've got to get out of here and draw this damned town's attention another direction before they find Charterhouse's animal. If there was ever a borned fool, here he sits!"

Time was short but he walked the pony twenty yards away from the slaughterhouse before applying spurs. He aimed east, veered and swept west. Presently he was facing the plaza from the sundown end and cracking bullets along the street to draw the embattled citizens away from the slaughterhouse and away from the direction Charterhouse had to go. The plaza was swarming with men; they came stumbling out of Studd's, out of the hotel, out of the dimly lit recess along the south side. Horses bunched; one stampeded crazily away. Guns answered, drawn by Seastrom's own flashing muzzle. Being a canny young man, he backed off beyond dangerous range, all the while watching the shadows.

"If Clint ain't hung up, he ought to be on his way by now," reflected the lone and somewhat bruised Box M puncher. "And I reckon I'll have to pull stakes and hike."

Heck started to cut around for the slaughterhouse again but saw he would never make it; a line of horsemen struck out from the plaza furiously and so wedged him off from that direction. He hauled about and raced for the southwest, worried and fretful. The pursuers had picked up his trail and were in stiff pursuit. Twice he started to curl off for the east and so reach the party in Bowlus' clearing; but each time he lost ground and found the others closing on him. So he settled down to run them out.

Meanwhile Clint Charterhouse, desperately trapped, had been granted a reprieve. Within two yards of a groping searcher, whose fingers were closing around the doorknob of the sheriff's office, he waited for the flood of light to come through. It was then the sudden shots from beyond the plaza broke like a warning gong. The searcher ripped open the door and plunged straight on through to the street without glancing back.

Those waiting in the rear of the jail broke for the nearest alley; and in the confusion Clint Charterhouse gambled on boldness. The sheriff's room was emptied; he pulled down his hat, ran through the room and gained the comparative darkness of the plaza, jostled by men to either side. Still in this human stream, he gained the stable, hurried through and settled for the slaughterhouse, vaulting over corral bars, going kneedeep in the slush of a water trough, and bruising himself badly against a wagon. But he gained the shed before others had begun to search that far from the buildings; and finding Seastrom's horse gone, he wasted no more time lining out for the ridge. The irrepressible Heck, he believed, had gotten into hot water and retreated according to instructions.

He set a fast pace, crossed the ridge, and hurried through the trees to the Bowlus clearing. Expecting guards to challenge, he slowed down. But there was no life in the clearing and no glimmer of light; he whistled softly, receiving only the echo for reply. Disturbed, he dismounted and poked his head into the cabin. After a tentative inspection he entered to try the bunk. But Bowles had disappeared, too.

Chapter TEN

Clint suspected a trap and retreated from the cabin in long, swift backward paces. Yet it appeared unreasonably strange that the trustworthy and matter-of-fact Fitzgibbon would pull away without powerful incentive. Striking around the cabin, Clint poked into the barn, angled across the meadow and came back to crouch down against the earth. Yet as the moments dragged by he heard only the sigh of the wind, the chant of the night creatures and the mysterious undertone of the prairie night. His own subtle senses, which he trusted so greatly, were quiescent; the meadow was empty. He went inside the cabin and ventured to strike a match, but the flare of light told him nothing. No signs, no apparent messages—nothing. Box M had departed, Bowlus had likewise gone, and Heck Seastrom was overdue.

Clint went out and climbed into the saddle, tarrying there with half-lifted reins while he turned the problem in his mind. Fitz might have decided to hit Shander a backhand wallop, he might have been driven off by a fresh attack from the renegades, he might have grown nervous and shifted ground, or he might have returned to Box M. None of these possibilities appealed to the fast-thinking Clint excepting the last. He recalled Haggerty's remark in the sheriff's office. Haggerty had been sent down to warn the Box M contingent. Whatever the warning and whoever had issued it, this empty meadow seemed to indicate Fitz had acted on its urgency and high-tailed for headquarters.

"Seems like straight thinking," opined Clint and gathered the reins. "A little queer, though, that Fitz didn't leave some word behind. Maybe he didn't want to expose his plans to some wandering Shander rider. Which is ex-

actly why I hadn't better leave a note for Heck. He'll have
to figure it out."

With that, he straightened down the meadow, let the
horse pick a path through the trees and a little later lined
across the open prairie for Box M. He regretted leaving
Seastrom on his own. But time pressed, the night was better than half gone and there was much riding yet to do.
As he clipped off the miles, he tried to piece together the
tag ends of information his eavesdropping behind the
sheriff's office had brought him. He had no idea where Fort
Carson was, nor what plan Shander and Curly had agreed
upon; but the fact that Curly had suggested a plan was
more or less an indication that they meant to smash Box
M hard and fast at some particular point. That was the
egotistic and impatient Curly's style.

"The piece of a licking they took tonight has sort of
brought things to a head," reflected Clint. "It's stung 'em.
They'll hit from the shoulder. Looks to me as if things
have smoked around to a downright spell of thunder and
lightning. As for Haggerty, I'm not much surprised. No
telling how much damage he's already done the ranch;
and he'll probably try to do a great deal more. If he
comes riding back, I can make a handy tool out of him, to
carry false hints. But I wonder if he'll come back?
Tonight's affair in Angels might have made him cagey."

So the intervening desert fell behind and Box M's shadowed outline loomed directly in front of him. No lights
broke over the earth; but his approach had been detected,
for he saw a silhouette cantering across his path. He
slowed and sent out a musical hail. In reply he was arrest-
ed bluntly.

"Draw in. Who is it?"

"Charterhouse."

"Come ahead slow. I don't make your voice."

The horses came face on. A Box M rider leaned cau-
tiously forward from his saddle and muttered, "Strike a
match." Clint obeyed. The guard relaxed, "Where's Seastrom?"

"He didn't show up and I didn't feel like there was time
to waste. Fitzgibbon pull in?"

"Yeah. Manners come back with twenty riders and we buried old John. Manners seemed to be plumb uneasy about something, for he told Sherry somebody had better ride towards Angels and draw Fitz back in case Shander made a strike at us. So Haggerty went to deliver the message. Why ain't he with you? He told Fitz he'd stay at the Bowlus place and wait for you and Heck."

"Who sent him away from the ranch?" pressed Clint.

"Why, I reckon he just took it upon himself to go," countered the other. "No—I call to mind Buck Manners pointed him out for the trip. Why ain't he with you?"

"You'll have to ask Haggerty next time you see him. What happened to Bowlus?"

"Fitz made him come in so's he wouldn't stop no stray lead."

Clint turned away and rode for the main house. Another guard came beside him and dropped away. He crossed the porch and went into the dark living room, calling quietly, "Sherry."

She was in an adjoining bedroom, but not asleep, for a quick answer came back. "Is it Clint? Wait there. I'll be right out."

Clint felt a chair in front of him and settled into it with a swift realization that he was extraordinarily tired. The events of the day had taken the sap out of him; and now that he let his mind play back upon them all the grim accidents flashed before him with a startling clarity and force. Compressed within sunrise and midnight was disaster, death, struggle and treachery; enough for an average life. Yet it was but the beginning. There was doubtless more to come, more death, more treachery and heartbreak and more weary hours of riding. His head slipped against the chair's tall back and his eyes, heavy with fatigue, dropped. When he started suddenly up to his feet, there was lamplight in the room and Sherry Nickum, tall and gravely beautiful in a bed robe, stood before him.

"You were dead to the world," she said softly. "I waited five minutes before I had the heart to waken you. Sam is outside. Let him put away your horse. You go to bed."

"Not yet."

"You have earned it, Clint."

"Maybe, but I doubt if any of us will be able to realize on our earnings in the next few days. Sherry, who sent Haggerty to bring Fitz's party back here?"

"Buck Manners came for . . . for the funeral, Clint. He had been to Angels and he seemed worried with what he saw there. He felt there was some bigger piece of trouble coming and he wanted me to draw in all the men to the place. I was not sure it was wise to interfere with your plans, Clint, and didn't exactly want to do it. But he insisted and overrode my objections. He told Haggerty to go—and go in a hurry. I'm sorry if it spoiled anything you had in mind."

"It might have," replied Clint somberly. "But I wasn't thinking of that. What time did Haggerty leave here?"

"Before sundown. Why?"

"I am just trying to settle a few queer items in my head," muttered Clint. "Is Manners here now?"

"He left for his place to get his crew posted. He thought the renegades might try to attack him, too. But he said he'd come back here before daylight himself."

Fitzgibbon, sleepy-eyed, tramped into the room. "Where's Seastrom and Haggerty?"

"Close the door, Fitz, and come over here."

Fitz did as he was told. Clint let his voice fall. "Seastrom and I got into Angels. I heard a few things. Seastrom was on the other side of town and I guess he got into trouble, for trouble developed. When I got back to my horse Heck had already pulled out. But he wasn't in the clearing and I couldn't wait for him. What did Haggerty tell you?"

"Why," reflected Fitz, "he told me to beat it for home in a hurry. I bucked, but he gave the orders in Sherry's name, so I couldn't do less. He said he'd stay and wait for you and Heck."

Clint calculated the hours swiftly. "So he left here at sunset and didn't reach you until after the scrap. That's around three-four hours he took to come on a trip that could be covered in an hour and a half or less of fast riding. I'd like to know where he detoured between the beginning and the finish."

"Yeah, but where is he?" asked Fitz. Both he and Sherry were watching Clint with aroused interest.

Clint trailed his voice to just above a whisper. "He didn't wait for me. He came into Angels and visited Studd, Curly and Shander. I was listening in. He's crooked! He's sold out. He's been on the other side of the fence for gosh knows how long. I think he tipped off our location in Bowlus' clearing to Curly and caused us to have a stiff battle. He might have been the instrument that would have wiped out Seastrom's party—only he didn't know that I had made a wide circle in the prairie and come down to back Seastrom up. I knew somebody in Box M would blab but I wasn't prepared to find Haggerty the man."

A small sigh escaped Sherry. Fitz, however, was too old a hand to display emotion. Nothing much surprised him and nothing much put him off balance. By and by he said, "It's possible. Anything's possible. He was a good foreman, but hard and sometimes uncivil."

Clint turned to Sherry. "Who was it that rode out of the yard right after I left with my party?"

"I didn't notice," said Sherry.

"Somebody did. There's more than one leak around here. Haggerty had some pets, didn't he?"

"A-huh," agreed Fitz.

"Then we'll have to keep an eye on them, too. Where's Fort Carson?"

"Fifteen miles toward Dead Man's Range. In fact, right in under Dead Man Ridge. Why?"

Clint walked suddenly to the door and opened it. But there was nobody on the porch. He came back. "Shander and Curly have agreed on some sort of a play over there tomorrow night. I don't know what, but I'm going to find out."

"Um," grunted Fitz. Clint held his peace while the stunted puncher followed some thought methodically to its end. "We got a spread of cattle that way."

"That might be it. Well, I'm going to line out in the

next ten minutes and hole up in some convenient arroyo
yonder. They won't get active until dark comes, but I'll
miss my guess if there won't be some sort of traffic during
daylight. I mean to see. You get me a fresh horse, will
you, Fitz?"

Fitz moved off. Clint added a swift—"and tell nobody
where I'm going."

Sherry broke in. "Not alone, Clint?"

"Only a one-man job," he countered. "I've found that I
work better alone on things like this."

"You're dead tired now."

"I'll get a catnap before daylight," he assured her.

She turned. "Come to the kitchen. You haven't eaten
since breakfast."

He followed her through the door into the gallery-like
kitchen. A small fire burned in the stove and the huge coffee pot simmered slowly, as it had done day and night for
unnumbered years in the ancient tradition of the ranch.
She poured him a cup and deftly robbed the cupboards to
make a meal. In the silence he watched her move about
the place—gracefully competent, features so sadly wistful.
The auburn hair fell loosely down over one temple; light
caught in the gray, level eyes when they turned his way,
and suddenly he looked down, tremendously disturbed.
She sat in a chair across the table while he ate, saying
nothing until he had quite finished. Then she tipped her
chin and spoke.

"You have always been lonesome, Clint? Always so sober with yourself?"

"A man goes along, doing what's to be done," he
drawled quietly. "When I was younger, I used to ride to
town with the boys, drink my share, create the customary
trouble, and come home with the idea I had spent a large
evening. That's being young, Sherry. It only comes
once—and goes soon enough."

"You talk like an old man, yet you haven't reached
twenty-eight."

"Now how did you know—"

A small, sad smile lightened the fine curve of her
mouth. "Because your eyes, your face, your voice give

you away. You only think youth is gone. That is because you have always taken responsibilities other men pushed off on you. Just as you are taking Box M's responsibilities now."

"I reckon I never was young," he mused. "Seems like I always had a job to do."

"Because others always found out you were able, Clint. Do you realize what it meant when Dad took so completely to you. Do you know what it means when the men of this ranch—all jealous of their own abilities—knuckle down to work for you?"

"Somebody's got to do it, Sherry."

"Yes, somebody. But not anybody."

Fitz came back, dragging his heels. "One of my own string out there for you, Clint. Now what else?"

"When dusk comes tomorrow evening," said Clint slowly, "you saddle twenty men of this outfit and burn the dust for Fort Carson. I'll be there waiting. And tell nobody where you're going. Nobody, Fitz."

"Remarks received and noted," grunted the old puncher.

The two men and Sherry moved back to the front room. Fitz had an idea. "Supposing Haggerty comes back, figuring he ain't been discovered. What then? Tie him up?"

"He won't come," said Clint. "That's my guess. But if he does, tell him I want him to ride with you. We shall see."

Fitz halted. But he saw something about these two people that changed his mind and he turned quietly out of the room. Sherry laid a hand on Clint's broad shoulder. "I have said this before, but it will bear repeating. Take good care of yourself."

He nodded, watching her. He was unaware that his face betrayed his inner emotions; but the girl saw something and she lifted her eyes to him with a strange flicker rising and subsiding in them. "And," she went on, "I will not change your plans again, nor order the men any other way than you already have. No matter what is said or who says it."

"I'll try to see you don't regret your confidence," said he. He stood quite still, swayed by the picture she made; it was with an effort that he wheeled, left the room and got on the horse. But out of ingrained caution Clint swept the shadows before lifting the reins and speaking. "She goes as she lays, Fitz. No matter what happens."

"A-huh," agreed the stolid Fitzgibbon.

Clint rode off, the horse beneath him restive with energy. As he turned the corner he looked around to see the girl framed in light, watching. She lifted her hand. He answered it, and fatigue strangely scurried out of him. Straight east he pointed and one hour later was lost in the rolling leagues; he dipped into an arroyo, dismounted and picketed his horse, himself rolling up in the saddle blanket on the rocky bed. Having achieved his immediate purpose, which was to get within striking distance of Fort Carson without being spied upon, he fell soon asleep. But it seemed only a moment later that he was wide awake and staring up to the paling stars in the sky. A horseman was drumming up from Box M direction; the man came abreast at a distance of about fifty yards and sped by, never veering. Clint saw the momentary blur of that rider's shadow from the rim of the arroyo, and he went back to his blanket extraordinarily thoughtful.

"Wonder if more information about me has leaked out? Seems like this country is shot with deceit. There goes a man in a mighty big hurry for Dead Man. A crook running to warn crooks. Appears—"

Far off, a lone shot's echo floated back, a signal in this mystery-ridden night. Clint shrugged his shoulders and slept again.

Buck Manners, riding alone and hurriedly, came into Box M quarters no more than a half hour after Clint pulled out. The yellow-haired ranch owner replied impatiently to the challenge of the guard and even more impatiently when he was halted again at the porch. "Fitz and the men back?" he asked.

"A-huh," said the guard.

"Everything go all right?"

"Was a scrap with Curly," said the guard. "We lost Pink, and Lee died on us later. But we put a worse crimp in Curly. Charterhouse come into the fight unexpected. That was his little surprise."

"The man is full of surprises," muttered Buck Manners. "I don't know that I approve of these brainstorms of his when they cost two men per throw."

There was a light burning in the living room, and Manners, knocking lightly, walked quickly in. Sherry sat in front of the fireplace with a blanket wrapped around her. Her troubled face turned to him and then dropped away. Manners pressed his lips together at this lack of interest. But he came over to warm his hands by the blaze, letting the silence run on for several minutes. Finally he drew himself straight.

"Sherry, you know me pretty well, don't you? I've been visiting Box M since I was one year old. You and I grew up together. You know the kind of a fellow I am—you've made up your mind about me long ago."

"I think so, Buck," she said slowly, still gazing into the flames.

"Then why in the name of heaven won't you let me take this burden off your shoulders? Look what is happening. All this fine scheming of Charterhouse's—"

"Don't belittle him, Buck. He walks with his head up and his heart clear."

"I have no desire to belittle the gentleman," explained Manners with a rather formal courtesy. "You know that is not my way. If I ever feel criticism for a man, I am willing to say as much to his face. I know nothing about Charterhouse's heart, but I think I've got a right to pick flaws in his judgment."

"He is fighting for this ranch, Buck."

"So indeed—but with what result? Two dead men and Curly's sure and certain revenge. It is poor tactics. It will not help Box M."

She lifted her eyes at that. "Then you know what had happened tonight?"

His easy-going carriage had been set aside; suddenly she saw clearly a part of his nature that hitherto had been suppressed—a part that she had sensed only in passing flashes. This Buck Manners was a dominant man, proud of his strength, a little grim, promising action. He spoke bluntly, the words striking clear and sharp in the room.

"I told you once that I could relieve you of all this burden. You saw fit to doubt it and put your trust in Charterhouse, a fellow who knows nothing of this country. It wasn't my place to explain what I could do. But I'll tell you now, Sherry, that I have more irons in the fire than you imagine. Nothing happens in this country I don't know of in short order. It's been pride with me. I have my own scouts out, my own men placed where they can do me the most good. That fight in the Bowlus meadow happened around nine o'clock. I knew of it one hour later. My dear girl, I *can* fight."

Her glance fastened more securely on him. "You have never hinted anything like this before, Buck. Did Dad ever know—"

He shook his head, and she thought he was regretting his confession. He went on doggedly. "It's been my hobby, a secret one. I have a great ranch, given to me without much work on my own part. But I have sweated and schemed and worked to establish some sort of underground supervision over Casabella. Those fools—Shander and the rest—don't know that I have their little tricky actions tagged and registered day by day. Frankly, Sherry, I have been content to collect information so far. For while your father lived I always regarded him as the boss of this county. But now, now that things have changed, I am moving into this struggle. I am going to boss Casabella, my dear girl. Before I get through they will jump through my hoop, or get out, or die!"

"Why, Buck, I never dreamed—"

He checked his swift eagerness. "Nor anybody else," he said more quietly. "I only tell you because I think you ought to let me do the fighting for you. I have tried to stand by and wait until this bitter business was gone from your heart. But I think we ought to be honest enough to look straight ahead. Sherry, I think you ought to marry me right away. I'd feel a thousand times easier, knowing

that you were where I could keep a better watch on you
and more protection around you. I could drive ahead
without worry. This is going to be a bad fight."

"Buck, I'm sorry—"

He was darkly displeased, struggling with temper. "So
you feel differently?"

A long silence. Her eyes fell away, a light in them
slowly withdrawing. "Yes," said she quite softly. "Yes,
I'm afraid so."

"Charterhouse?"

"I—I don't know, Buck."

"I do," he grunted. "Better if the man had never seen
this country."

She had a swift answer for that. "Buck, you must not
turn against him now! You're not a mean man, not small.
You'll back him up—you must."

"Take my licking and grin, is that it? Sherry, you don't
know me so well if you think it's that easy. I have waited
a long time for you. I'd rip this country end to end to
keep you. I fight for the things I've won. Let Charterhouse show he's fit to have you."

"No, Buck. You don't mean that. You will be his
friend. You've got to be."

The anger and the stiffness went out of him suddenly
and after a long interval he nodded his blond head.
"Yeah, I suppose. Grin and wish him luck. I have never
taken a licking in my life but now I've got to take the
worst of all. There never was a man who could match my
muscle till he came along. He smiled when he did it, and I
could have used the gun on him for that. Sherry, I've got
my weaknesses. Some you've never seen. Pride, ambition.
Here he comes and cuts the ground from under me without lifting his voice. Lord. I never thought any man on
earth would do it to me."

"But you'll be his friend, Buck?"

"Yeah," he muttered dryly. "Much as it's possible to
be."

She switched the subject. "You've heard about Haggerty?"

His interest flashed up sharply. "What about him?"

She seemed to debate something in her mind. "He—hasn't come back yet."

"That's all?" he demanded, studying her.

"No-o. Clint managed to get into Angels and overheard Haggerty talking with Shander and Studd and Curly. Haggerty's crooked, Buck."

"Crooked? I don't believe it! Well, hold on. It may be so at that. Haggerty's not an open-handed man. Funny streak in him. You're sure about it?"

"Clint heard too much to doubt it."

"That means there may be others about the ranch then," muttered Manners. "You'll have to be careful. Keep your crew on hand all the time. Don't let them go on any wild-goose chases. You weren't planning on any attack, were you?"

She stared at the fire thoughtfully; and committed her first deliberate evasion. "I don't know what Clint's plans are."

"You trust him too much," fretted Manners. "Where is he now?"

"He took a fresh horse—" admitting it reluctantly, "and rode toward Dead Man alone."

Manners rolled a cigarette. Silence came over the broad room; these two people, so long friends, so long without secrets, were slowly drifting apart. A heavy wall of constraint fell between them.

Manners spoke sadly. "See, you don't even trust me as you once did. When it comes to that pass, Sherry, the old times are gone. Yet you ask me to like Charterhouse and support him, even when I doubt his wisdom and know nothing of his past. And there's nothing for me to do but say I will. Whatever happens, any time, any place, you only have to call and I'll come. A sorry ending, after all I'd hoped. Let it be so. I'm riding home."

He strode for the door and was on the verge of passing out before her answer caught and stopped and turned him. "I had not meant to break off our engagement, Buck. Not tonight. I wasn't sure of myself. I couldn't decide. Yet in the past five minutes I know it best. Only—you won't think bad of me because of it, will you?"

"I'd be a putty man if I said it didn't hurt, if I didn't want to fight this thing out and make somebody suffer. But there will never be a time in my life when I don't consider you the sweetest, finest—"

He broke off. She saw him then as she was never to see him again. The lamplight reached out to touch his slim, symmetrical body. The corn-yellow hair was a little disheveled, and his clothes were dusty; but he stood there a man, vital instincts surging in him, eyes flashing, and all his features set in fighting lines. A gentleman of the land, every inch. The door closed and he was in the saddle and the drum of his pony's flying hoofs came rhythmically back, fading into the eastern edge of the world. Sherry's small hands gripped the arms of the chair as she listened, and her cheeks paled perceptibly. In that headlong tempo of a man and beast there was something ominous, something dreadfully disturbing.

Chapter ELEVEN

In the rolling mists that preceded dawn, Clint Charter-house woke from his short sleep and moved on to the east. Desert cold cut through his clothes, the stars glimmered frostily and the slim silver crescent of the moon began to fade slowly from the sky. Visibility increased by slow degrees as he traveled—still keeping to the arroyos that ran into one another all the way toward Dead Man's Range.

The range itself was a darkling, irregular bulk in the foreground, but Clint paid it scant attention; more immediately interesting was the nearing outline of Fort Carson, a deserted and empty relic of the Indian fighting days. It made a very good tenement for the lawless band troubling Casabella. Clint half suspected Curly's men to be hidden in those small frame buildings that ranked evenly all the way around a rectangular parade ground; yet he rose from the protection of the arroyo and came flanking in toward the fort for a closer view.

This last hour of the night was a time when almost all men slept, no matter what danger confronted them and no matter what devices they might be up to; it was the lax hour, the hour of low ebb in courage and vitality. So he drifted quietly along a lane of poplar trees leading to the parade ground and stopped in the convenient gloom created by one of them.

From his post he looked directly upon the buildings, the offset barns and sheds. To one side were the larger buildings—company barracks, he surmised—in a crumbling state of disrepair; to the other sat those smaller, neater houses meant for officers and their families. Some of these, too, were sagging at hip and eave, and their doors and porches were ripped away by passing punchers in need of wood for fire; yet other structures seemed to have been kept up. But nowhere did he see a horse, nowhere a sign of present occupancy. As a matter of self-interest he trailed his horse all about the fort and looked at it from opposite angles.

"Deserted," he mused. "Curly figures it too exposed a place to camp. He must be hiding in the hills."

Light was perceptibly creeping over Dead Man and filtering through the desert gloom, the fog dissipating. The world would be awake presently and hidden men again be on the watch; so Clint took up his march for the hills, reached the bench land within fifteen minutes and filed up a rocky, barren draw. At an elevation of about five hundred feet he found himself in a maze of bowls, pinnacles, rock cairns and animal trails. From his vantage point he surveyed the western flatlands rise through the fog. Leaving his horse in a depression, he went back to the rim and swept the scene with careful attention. Dawn suddenly surprised the world; the eastern light grew stronger and then the first shaft of the sun streamed like a golden banner over the prairie, bringing all objects into view with startling clarity; at about the same moment Clint saw two or three riders dusting out of the southwest—from the direction of Shander's.

He rolled a cigarette contemplatively while time passed. "Bit by bit this crooked scheme coils tighter," he reflected. Here's a fine, bright day which was meant for men to enjoy; yet if ever hunches played me right, these next twelve hours will be Casabella's worst memory for years to come. And those fellows yonder open up the ball."

They swung on their course and pointed for Fort Carson. Three of them loping along at their ease. Clint waited stolidly as the sun began to beat upon his back and all the crisp freshness of the small hours was sucked out of the air by the burning ball of fire riding up the sky. The riders quested into the fort parade ground and were temporarily lost. Ten minutes later they emerged and came straight on for what Clint recognized from description to be Dead Man Range. Clint ran his eyes along the foot of the hills carefully. A main road seemed to cut directly into Dead Man Ridge a mile south of his location, and this road the three riders too, presently going around a shoulder and disappearing.

Clint hitched up his belt and started afoot across the rough terrain. It was confusing country and a little way off he turned to identify the bowl in which his horse was hidden; then he pressed on, rising and falling with the rugged pitch. Dead Man was a naked, treeless ridge with a series of spines divided by deep depressions; thus it was Clint had only a partial view of the country immediately about him. Going to the south, he came upon a round and grassy bowl fit to hold fifteen or twenty head of cattle compactly; skirting it, he observed the charred circle of an old campfire at the bottom.

But he refused to go down for a closer look. Taking to a runway gouged out by winter's rain, he fell into a jog trot until warned by a blank cliff ahead that he was nearly arrived at the main pass.

He left the runway, angled for a more rocky stretch and flattened himself full length on the ground, shoulders between a widely split stone and chin almost hooked over the rim of the pass. Some distance below and eastward the three riders had halted to confront a fourth who seemed to have made his appearance from the southward reaches of Dead Man. This was Curly, white face visible beneath the ipped hat; the others had their backs to Clint, but he thought he recognized Studd by the man's bulky torso. They were gesturing freely. The restless Curly kept cutting the air with his quirt and his horse shifted. Then all four had veered and faced a fissure leading into the pass as another man rode quickly down into view and halted them. Clint half rose and fell back with a long sigh of pure astonishment. His eyes narrowed and all his muscles tightened up.

"Good gosh, who will it be next? I don't believe this, but it must be so."

All five stood in a circle. The parley kept on for a quarter hour, at the end of which time the fifth man turned

abruptly and disappeared whence he had emerged. Curly
made a swashbuckling circle in the air with his arm and
climbed a southward trail; the original three turned down
the main road, backtracking for the prairie. When they
rode directly beneath Clint, he recognized them all—
Studd, Shander and Haggerty. As long as he had sight of
them he waited, then rose and cut back for his original
point of observation. At that location he rolled another
cigarette and settled down to long watchfulness and grim
reflection.

"Farther I go into this mess the worse it gets. But what
in hell is the reason behind all this?"

The three had reached the fort again and were up to
something. One man pulled away and galloped in a
looping course toward Angels. "Must be Shander, going
home," Clint reflected. "But it might be Studd or Haggerty hitting into town. Now what?"

The crack of a shot came thinly back. A second rider
turned the fort and spurred due north, paralleling the
ridge and closing upon it. Clint watched him until the
man had gone around the curve of the bench land; but
there was ample this bright morning to keep his attention
occupied. A line of horsemen streamed down from the re-
cesses of Dead Man a few miles south of Clint's position
and aimed for the fort. As they arrived there, the party
split into fragments and scattered over the prairie, heading
toward Box M.

"Light begins to dawn," said Clint. "They're looking
into the arroyos. Who for? Me. Somebody got wind of my
whereabouts and squealed. Worse and worse. How is a
man to make a move against Shander under such circumstances? Hell."

Far off a rider popped from the earth and came along;
a similar miracle happened at a more northerly point of
the horizon. Clint shook his head dubiously. "Scouts.
Probably been posted in gopher holes all night. Or all
week, for that matter. Who knows? I begin to see the ram-
ifications of this system. An almost unbeatable play."

The morning passed slowly. Noon came. Curly's men

were so many dark points moving restlessly over the
chrome-yellow prairie, cutting endless circles and tangents.
Later they shifted, converged into a solid group. Apparently a trail had been struck, for the group pounded back,
flanked the fort once and stretched out for Dead Man's
Range, aiming squarely at Clint. He shifted on the
ground, lips tightening. "Got a smell of me. Well, it will
do them no good. I can play tag in this stuff all day long."

Apparently the party arrived at the same conclusion. At
the foot of the bench it halted, sent out desultory searchers to right and left and waited. The baked soil gave up
nothing; Clint's pony tracks had petered out on hardpan
and rock. By and by the party swung back. Clint relaxed.
Some sort of communication was being established with
Shander's ranch, for a rider came rapidly up from that direction, laying a thin ribbon of dust to his rear. At about
the same time another rider hurried from the fort and
drove straight for the main pass of Dead Man. Clint calculated all these with puzzled attention; somebody yonder
was in a big sweat. Apparently a great many strings had
to be pulled together.

"Don't know much more than I did in the beginning,"
he soliloquized. "But I've got to figure this thing out
straight or make an awful bobble. According to what I
heard last night, they mean to make some sort of play
around here this evening. Now, it's leaked out that I'm in
these parts. They figure I possibly know what they aimed
to do. Therefore, they won't do it. They'll do something
else. Or will try? That's a question. Clint, my boy, you'd
better get the right answer before the shades of night fall
thick and fast. If they don't go through with the original
business, what might they do, and where would they do
it? Sounds like the talk of a crazy man—"

Activity slackened off yonder as the afternoon went
along and the sun slanted into the west. It was siesta time,
when the cycle of life reached its second lethargic stage.
In spite of himself, Clint drowsed a little, eyes half closed
against the glare and his mind worrying away on his problem. The patient pony moved around the depression; Clint

swept the rutty area of the ridge behind him and once more took up his post. He thought he saw something away off in Box M direction and pulled down the brim of his hat for a fairer view.

Thus, by the flash of a second and the rise of an arm, did he miss catching sight of an object that rose from cover and quickly fell back, about three hundred yards to his right rear. A little later Driver Haggerty's sour, stringy face lifted above the rocks again and fastened on the unwarned Charterhouse. In the man's look was a coldness and the unwinking directness of a reptile.

Over a period of fully five minutes he remained in this motionless posture, only his glance swinging from Charterhouse to the rocks near by. It were as if he thoroughly weighed every possibility and entrapping circumstance that might defeat his objective. Having satisfied himself, he rolled his body around to study the country whence he had come. His horse was a quarter mile off and though there was a rifle in the saddle boot—for men of Casabella never rode without long arms—it was too much of a trip to return and get the gun. It would have to be a matter of revolvers.

Not that Haggerty regretted the choice; in many ways he was a patient man, extraordinarily so where his private vengeance was concerned. Finding Charterhouse had not been accident; early in the morning he had learned of Charterhouse being around Fort Carson, and while Curly elected to scour the prairie, he had posted along the ridge, entered a convenient draw and gained the top. His own theory was that if Charterhouse still remained anywhere near the fort, it would be in a position of some worth, both high enough to scan the country and near enough to the fort to observe what went on. Being shrewd himself and very tricky, he credited Charterhouse with the same kind of ability.

Therefore, he had started away north on the ridge and advanced by tentative, guarded stages, always hugging the rim. Nothing could have demonstrated his stolid, Indian-like fixity of purpose more clearly; he had started at sunrise of the day and all through the intervening hours he had stalked onward. It was now four o'clock or better. A small sigh of satisfaction came out of his thin lips. Lifting his body with the sinuousness of a lizard, he half rolled and half pitched into the next pothole.

Again the whole weary business of inching to the rock rim and peering ahead took place; and again he slid ahead to cut down the distance between. But as Charterhouse seemed wholly absorbed in the prairie scene, Driver Haggerty grew more confident. He swung, got behind a vast granite thumb protruding to the sky, slipped into an arroyo and went slinking along it for a full fifty yards. When he popped up again he was directly behind Charterhouse, and the intervening distance had diminished by half. Now Haggerty, utilizing every possible obstruction, wriggled forward, stopping, staring, listening, and proceeding. He threw aside his hat and wiped his stringy jaws, down the furrows of which fresh springing sweat kept coursing. Deeper crimson swelled the habitually dark skin; his eyes burned. A hundred yards removed, he halted and took a fresh chew of tobacco, discovering he had, in the course of all this belly marching, badly bruised and cut his hands. The downsweep of his saturnine mouth grew more pronounced; and he inched forward.

He was within possible revolver range when the first doubt came over him. Charterhouse had scarcely moved a muscle in the last twenty minutes; the man seemed to be welded to the earth. Sleeping? The possibilities brought Haggerty's features into sudden wolfish angles. His eyes stung with sun-glare, and though he dropped them and looked at the ground to relieve the pressure, there were little flecks of black blurring his vision. He brought up his gun, braced his elbows and took a test sight. Ordinarily he would have felt certain of bringing down any sort of game at this distance. But the tension, the blur constantly before him, and the strain of knowing that there might never be chance for a second shot caused him to lower the gun and roll into the next pothole. When he arrived at the rim of this one, he saw Charterhouse's hidden horse. He settled there, determined to go no farther; bringing up the gun, he saw a jagged hole in Charterhouse's coat below the neck and between shoulder points. Cold as ice inside, Driver Haggerty brought down his sights and lined them on the hole.

It was a good target, a good distance. It was nothing more than a swift off-hand draw. Yet Haggerty, swearing at his doubt and his puzzlement, swearing even at his unnecessary deliberation, squinted along his sights, lowered his gun, wiped his palms dry, and tried again. Deliberation seemed to throw him off; he had trouble bringing the muzzle into center—he who was able to skip a tomato can along the prairie. Squeezing down the trigger slack, a greater doubt than all before actually chilled him. He tipped the muzzle another time and twisted his neck, looking behind, fearing to see himself trapped. But nothing but barren surface was there, and venomously angry, he turned to his gun to make a quick shot.

Charterhouse stirred, brought up an elbow and started to roll on his back.

That ruined Haggerty's long, careful focus; in one wild prompting of rage he discarded all his deliberateness, leaped to his feet and flung a free shot at the now warned Charterhouse; the latter was still turning and the sight of Haggerty standing above, drawn and grim and with the killing lust flaming in those round red eyes, served to accelerate Charterhouse's movements. The bullet missed its mark by the thickness of paper, chipping up rock fragments. Still on his back, still rolling, Charterhouse drew on the tall plain bulk of the foreman and fired. The hammer fell on Haggerty's second shot, but Charterhouse's bullet had set the foreman back on his heels and his slug went high over Dead Man's rim and on down into the bench.

Haggerty trembled at the knees and his yellowish face paled. The clack of his tongue, trying to frame a word, sounded across the stillness of that dying afternoon and a shield of blood widened, ragged and ghastly, on his shirt front. Then pain screwed the man's face into a terrible grimace, and he fell forward, pitching down into the sharp bottom of the depression, rolling to the very feet of the shifting horse. He was dead before his lank body had stopped turning.

Charterhouse, badly shaken, sprang across the depression and stood up to view the back stretch of the ridge. He half expected to find more men rising to sight. But there were none and as his mind raced swiftly along, he knew that silent and tedious advance could mean only that Haggerty had tried to do the job single-handed. He stared at the foreman, without pity, without regret. In fact, his thoughts pulled away from the incident and settled on thought of consequences that might develop from the sound of those three shots beating out from the ridge and down to the fort. Going back to his point of view, he discovered men riding out from the parade ground slowly, seeming to be interested but not alarmed. The sun was sinking away in the west; shortly purple twilight would sweep like a veil over the prairie.

"And nothing decided yet," muttered Charterhouse.

For him, nothing had been decided. But he believed Curly and the allied renegades had hit upon their future course. The long inactivity was broken by a rider who streamed out from a distant angle of the ridge. He reached the fort and within fifteen minutes that same rider, or another, went beating away toward Angels. Shots echoed back, evenly spaced, and presently men appeared from afar and loped in. It reminded Clint of a bivouacked army drawing back its sentries prior to marching. The sun sank; twilight came, remained but an uncertain moment and deepened to darkness. Clint sighed and rose. He pulled his horse from the depression, mounted, and without so much as a glance back at the dead foreman, went down the ridge into the prairie. There was a light shining from the fort when he flanked it at the distance of a mile, but as he shot onward toward Box M to intercept Fitzgibbon, the light went out. Unbroken darkness, unbroken mystery settled down.

Once more the night wind murmured of things hidden; and although Clint Charterhouse was not an overly imaginative man, he reflected that on the wings of that breeze were all the voices of Casabella's dead warning him of wrath to come. The old, old story was about to repeat itself; across the sands was to be written another lurid chapter in bloody ink. Casabella politics.

Chapter TWELVE

If Fitz had obeyed orders—and Charterhouse believed that puncher was an utterly trustworthy wheelhorse—the Box M party was now halfway on the road to Fort Carson; so he increased the pace of his tired pony, stopping every few minutes to listen for the reverberation of hoof beats. Even yet he had not made up his mind; even yet Curly's movements puzzled him. All that he had overheard in Angels tended him to the belief that the renegades meant a play around Fort Carson. Logically this would be a raid on Box M beef and a drive into the secrecy of Dead Man Range. Out of his own knowledge Charterhouse understood there could be no easier way of picking a fight and of drawing a Box M posse after the missing stock and thus opening up a battle. He had thought this was what Curly meant to do.

But Curly had ridden toward Angels with his whole party, a move that bore no relation to the Box M cattle in the north. It was probable that Curly might have figured the game was up—that he, Charterhouse, had overheard the plan in Angels—and was preparing for it. Such being so, what then would the renegades do?

"Something, that's sure," reflected Clint. "There was entirely too much riding in and out of Dead Man, too many messengers covering the country to Shander and Angels and back. That outfit is pitched to fight, and when a scope of hard suckers get on their ears, they'll strike one way if they can't strike another. There's been a leak from the ranch. They knew I was riding. They may even know Fitz is bringing most of Box M's strength away from home quarters. Then the thing for them to do would be to circle around us and smash right into old John Nickum's front yard. They might be doing it this minute."

143

He had reasoned out the situation accurately. He knew he had. Yet through all his thinking there was one qualifying, uncertain shadow of doubt—the fifth man at the morning meeting of outlaws in Dead Man's Pass. That man rode through all plans, all guesses, all probabilities. And so when Clint stopped and caught the approach of horsemen, he had very nearly reached a mental deadlock. The party swept on vigorously. Clint cut to the right to intercept them. They bore down, a compact and growing blur against the velvet curtain; fresh horses and fresh men hitting a stiff gait. He waited until his natural voice would reach them and then sent out a soft challenge. "Fitz?"

The party swirled around him, reining in noisily. Fitzgibbon's voice answered, as imperturbable and laconic as ever. "Yeah. Charterhouse? All right. We in time?"

Another voice broke through—Heck Seastrom's. "Hell's fire, Charterhouse, you wait until we can swap lies! I got a story to tell, damned if I ain't. Now where to?"

"This bunch feels heavier than twenty men," remarked Charterhouse.

"Yeah," agreed Fitz. "Thirty-one of us. I got to thinking and so did Sherry. Whole hog or none. We know Casabella pretty well, Charterhouse. And Manners sent over four fellows to stick around the place, late this afternoon. So Sherry kept four more of our bunch and told me to bring the rest along."

"So Manners is supporting Box M?" drawled Charterhouse.

"A-huh. What's next?"

Charterhouse spoke quietly. "I just want you boys to know it is a gamble. I've watched Curly's outfit play around Carson all day long and don't know any more than I did this morning. He pulled out just before dark, heading for Shander's. Leaving the fort empty. He may be circling to hit Box M, or he may be laying down a screen of dust for himself. But there's just one item in my mind that decides me to gamble. I want you to know it before we ride back to Carson and hole up there. And wait for Curly to return. That's the plan."

"I might give you some information," broke in Seastrom. "I dragged hell's-half acre getting home from Angels. Had to do a lot of dodging this morning; and I was in an arroyo south of Shander's when that gentleman breezed by with his fifteen hands. They seemed to be making a big curve in the prairie for the lower tip of Dead Man."

Charterhouse considered it, putting together the stray pieces of the puzzle. A more definite snap came to his words. "That helps, Heck. It is still a gamble. I am taking all the responsibility for failure. That's all I'll say. Any objections?"

"You're the boss," muttered Fitzgibbon.

"Lead off," put in Seastrom. "One man's guess is as good as another in this country and you seem to guess pretty lucky. Bust the breeze."

"Come on, then," snapped Charterhouse and turned in front of them.

The party gathered speed behind. Fitz was to his left, Seastrom to the right and chuckling softly as if it were some thundering fine midnight party. The stars winked clear and the crisp air fanned against them, carrying the pungency of sage and earth into their nostrils. Leather squealed and the jingle of those many bridle chains made a pleasant melody. Fort Carson broke the distance and presently the avenue of poplars loomed dead ahead. Charterhouse slowed to a walk, pressed on a few yards and halted.

"Seastrom—three men. Down the left side afoot. Three more with me to the right. Fitz, wait with the bunch. If there's a bust of guns, use your ears and judgment, but I think the place is still empty.

There was a soft dismounting and a swift filing off. Seastrom and his followers faded into the blur made by the line of officers' quarters. Clint swung to the opposite side and stopped at an open door of a barrack while his men overshot him and pressed on in quick, sure silence. No sound came out of the building, no warning of crouched danger. Satisfied, he struck directly down the parade and closed upon the outlying sheds. Nothing here; turning, he saw one of Heck's searchers slide rapidly up.

"Clear?"

"I think so."

"Go back and tell Fitz to come along."

Standing there, Clint thought he heard the tremor of moving bodies come along the air; he dropped to the ground. The invisible telegraph was alive, beating out its message, strengthening with each moment. He rose, hurrying back. Fitz led in the party. Charterhouse's word ran together, electric and urgent. "They're coming in. Hustle it, boys. Everybody out of the saddle and into the houses on the east side of the parade ground. Run the horses into that end shed—four men to hold 'em. String out a little so you've all got a good place to sling lead. Hustle it, now. And no firing until you hear me sing out."

"They're sure coming," grunted Fitz briefly.

"Here's where some of them handpicked lilies wilt on the stem," added Heck, strangely subdued. "Man, here's a scrap."

"I'm afraid so," said Charterhouse. "Lets clear out of this plaza. No shooting, boys, until I sound the word."

Standing with his back to a house wall, he listened to the renegades sweep out of the distance and bear down. And in that lull he reviewed the past days with a queer clarity—old John Nickum dying bravely, the savage growl of Angels, all that trickery, all the vengeance of predatory men seeking to destroy and rob, the glistening evil in Shander's sickly eyes and the animal remorselessness of this callow Curly who advanced so hurriedly. All these facts and scenes flashed across Clint's mind, telling him as a thousand cold words could not that whatever happened this night was only the march of inevitable events, only the blossoming of that deadly flower—hate.

And while Clint's muscles tightened expectantly and his nerves slowly chilled and left him like a thing of stone, he still had time for regret. Men would fall. Good men and bad men. Lives that had so long savored God's fresh sun, keened the crispness of the prairie air, and moved in the vast, heady freedom of this open land, would be snuffed out in the roar of shots. What would be, would be. This was the price paid for safety and orderly justice. In the west it had always been so. Men who lived by the gun died by the gun. Defying all order and transgressing all rules of right, they courted death—and so would they receive it. And with that thought Clint Charterhouse settled his conscience and closed his mind.

A lesser man would have trembled and sickened; a man from a gentler country would have shuddered, flinched away. But all Clint's forefathers had struggled with the same problem from one frontier to another; his thinking was molded by the brutally clear and direct logic of the time. Men had to stand by and be responsible for their acts; men had to pay their bills. That was the whole story. Some day these things would not be, but for the present the rough-handed code prevailed. And he was of that large-boned, tough-fibered fighting type that, once having decided the course, moved ahead relentlessly. A son of the west.

The renegades pounded on, curving around the fort. Charterhouse, frozen against the wall, thought they were sweeping by and started to readjust his plan of battle. But it was only a sort of scouting movement. They circled, swung and started into the plaza from the north side. Heck Seastrom stirred slightly and Charterhouse heard the methodical Fitzgibbon sigh very softly. Curly's men filed past, slackened and bunched up. Men and horses made an irregular bulk out there. For a moment absolute silence reigned, broken at last by the voice of Curly.

"Well, Shander?"

"We'll wait a minute," replied Shander.

"I don't see why we been doing all this fool back and forward moving around the prairie. We've lost a lot of time. It's eight miles to Box M cattle and there'll be a hard ride into Dead Man with 'em. The night ain't so young, either."

"We'll wait a minute."

A few, soft phrases came from Curly, at which Shander

sharply checked him. "Never mind. You know what I'm waiting for, but keep it under your tongue."

Heck punched Charterhouse in the ribs, and Charterhouse saw men in the rear of Curly's bunch shift. An uneasy sentence ran along the entire line. "Say, ain't there horses up yonder? I thought I heard—"

Charterhouse took a pace forward and spoke, each word falling flatly. *"You're trapped. Give in—or fight!"*

"By God—!"

The night was streaked suddenly by tangled shadows as Curly's bunch broke, wheeled and raced for protection. A gun flash mushroomed out and then a long and ragged volley smashed into Fort Carson's walls, disturbing the long sleeping ghosts of fighters dead and gone. Charterhouse was on his stomach, crying, *"Let them have it—let them have it!"* and Box M's solid, blasting reply overbore the echoes of that first fire from the renegades. Curly had gone stark mad, his yells shrill as those of a woman, unprintable and weird. He seemed to be beating back one of his own followers, forcing him from flight. Others were in a milling mass near the sheds; Box M men had run out from shelter to cut off retreat that way.

Curly yelled again. "Charterhouse—damn your soul! Stand out and meet me! Where are you—where are you?"

Charterhouse stood up. "Come ahead, Curly."

Lead smashed into the wall behind him like hail. Glass jangled and there was a ripping of wood. A horseman wheeled and aimed at him. It was Curly, still cursing. Charterhouse met the man with point-blank bullets; the horse swerved, suddenly riderless and got tangled in the porch rail of an adjoining house. Other ponies, saddles empty, were stampeding around the empty plaza. Curly's men were badly split up; a part of them had dismounted and were fighting from individual coverts; another part, taking whatever leadership offered, rode over to a barrack across the plaza and tumbled inside.

Charterhouse called at Heck. "Pick up a few boys and get behind that thing. That's just the sort of a cage I want 'em in." And then, knowing the dispiriting power of a leader's death, he flung his words out into the frenzied plaza. "Curly's dead! Come on, Box M, crush those snipers! Get around—flank 'em—pour the lead!"

"Curly's dead!"

Three of the renegades, still mounted and boxed in one corner of the plaza, seemed to lose reason. They flung themselves diagonally over the open space and drove for liberty. Charterhouse fired; other guns roared in his ears, and he saw a saddle emptied. The other two got past. There was a wicked slash of bullets down by the shed as the two survivors tried for the prairie and then another horse galloped aimlessly back without guidance. Box M was tasting victory. Punchers sallied out of their protection and alternately ducked and scurried over to smother the isolated snipers along the barracks. Heck was shouting tempestuously, "Come over here, Box M—we got this shebang tied in knots! Come on, you scorpions!"

Charterhouse ran across toward Heck's gang. A shadow leaped at him, missed and went by. He flung himself to the ground, dust in his face, feeling lead strike around his head. A sharp crack and a strangled cry—and Fitzgibbon was talking calmly.

"Hurt, Charterhouse?"

"No."

"You hadn't oughta be so brash. Watch out!"

Another pair of riders elected to fight clear, flashing out from the shadows. Hoofs grazed Charterhouse, a dangling stirrup knocked him down, and from the prairie came a long halloo of defiance. He got up and labored with his wind. A gun popped here and there, but the madness of the initial shock was dying. Seastrom yelled again for reinforcements. Some battle between individuals flared by the horse sheds and stopped abruptly. The snipers were quitting, some captured, some beyond capture, and some wriggling out to the prairie afoot. Box M began to concentrate on the barrack containing the bulk of Curly's gang. Charterhouse caught one of his men by the arm.

"Rip down some planks and start a fire here. A husky one to see by." Then he closed on the barrack and called out. "Slack off, Box M. Hold your lead. You Curly men—it's all over. Don't try to make a stand. We've got you crushed. Curly's dead. Throw down your guns."

Silence descended. Somewhere a man groaned and somewhere else was a bitter cursing. Out of the barrack came a sullen, tentative proposal.

"You fellows guarantee us a free ride to the county line, and we'll come."

"Guarantee nothing."

"We don't aim to step out and be shot down. We'll either get unhindered passage over the line or else we'll fight it out. We know Casabella politics."

The Box M man had accumulated his tinder-dry boards and some sort of kindling material. He struck a match, applied it, and sprang away. In dead silence the assembled punchers watched the fitful spiral of fire sputter, fall and catch hold. Charterhouse spoke again. "There will be no lynching and no shooting. Either surrender or else."

"Or else what?" jeered the voice. "We can punch some holes in you buzzards yet. Go to hell."

"You'll go to hell in a crackling blaze," said Charterhouse. "See this little bonfire? If I put one of these burning planks against that barrack, you won't live fifteen minutes."

The trapped renegades debated. The spokesman tried again. "Well, what if we come out?"

"You are going to Angels and sleep in the jug until Box M gets ready either to put you on trial or kick you out of the county. It's apt to be the second choice, considering the state of jury trials in this neck of the woods."

"Your word for that?"

"My word for it."

"Ain't worth a hell of a lot," grumbled the spokesman.

"No? Well, it's the best you got on the subject, brother. This fire is getting large and comfortable."

"All right, we'll come."

Charterhouse motioned to the nearest Box M men to stand beside the barrack door. "All right, inside. Pop out one at a time, elbows stiff. Heck, you herd these brutes into shape. Better snag a rope around 'em somehow."

"Just leave that to me," agreed Heck.

Charterhouse skirted the leaping fire and walked back toward the sheds. Other Box M men were poking through the shadows, swearing morosely. One of them called toward the sheds. "Ain't there an old flat-bed wagon in there? Used to be."

"Yeah. What for?"

"What for? What in damnation you think for? For them that's past walking, of course. Drag it out. We can hook onto the tongue and haul it home with ropes."

Charterhouse felt weary. And when he saw a sprawled, still body in front of him he reached for his matches sadly. The single flare of light told him all he wanted to know. There lay all that remained of the swashbuckling, vainly immature savage known as Curly. A short life— and nothing to show for it but a stain of blood on the earth. Fitzgibbon, some yards off, had repeated the performance, and announced his discovery with an unusual departure from matter-of-factness. "Great Guns—Shander!"

"The roll of the crooked," muttered Charterhouse. "He was riding at the head of the party and caught the worst of the fire." Rather bitterly he summed up that rancher's career. "He had his range and he wanted more. Now he's got just six feet of it left." Sitting on a porch, he reviewed the scene before him. Seastrom was herding the surrendered party into a long row by the revealing rays of the fire. Suddenly he called out. "Hey, Clint, do you know we've got Mister Shander's riders here, too? Kit and caboodle. A clean sweep. Gents, I'm pleased to see you at this party. Nothing would suit me better than to see the bottom of your boots kicking the breeze. Being we're civilized folks, I reckon it ain't to be. But, by gosh, I'd like to—and you know my sentiments on the subject once for all." Half a dozen men were wheeling the flat-bed wagon toward the fire; somebody came by the flames with an armful of saddle blankets and Charterhouse saw the man's face furrowed and wet. Crying—

Clint stirred. Curly and Shander and Haggerty gone. Of the ringleaders known to the county only Studd and Wolfert remained. The back of the crooked bunch was broken.

And yet this grim piece of business was unfinished. Would never be finished until that last showdown came with the man who—

Seastrom came over the plaza, calling, "Clint—hey, Clint. We're set to ride. What next?"

"How do we stand?"

Seastrom cleared his throat. "I reckon we'll have to add Ed Porn and Lou Lester to our boot hill. Dammit all, it's tough; I knew these two fellows like brothers. But I reckon they're riding a better range now. It's a chance we all take, ain't it?"

"So," mused Charterhouse.

"I figure about ten of the wild bunch got away. That won't bother us any. They'll keep running until Casabella's damn far off. I know. As for them that had hard luck—"

"Put them in a building and leave them till morning," cut in Charterhouse abruptly. "We'll be back then to see they get a decent burial. Now, Heck, you take part of the outfit and ride down to Angels with your herd. Stick 'em in the calaboose and if you see Studd or Wolfert there, do the same with those gentlemen. And rule the town until further orders."

"Nothing I look forward to with more pleasure," grunted Seastrom.

Fitz came out of the deeper darkness. "You take the rest of the fellows, and the wagon, and strike for home," Clint told him.

"Where you going?" Seastrom wanted to know.

"I'm staying here for a few minutes to think about it," droned Clint. "Well, you might as well hit the trail."

Both Fitz and Seastrom hesitated, seeming to study out the meaning of Charterhouse's voice. Presently, without answer, they walked across the plaza. Charterhouse watched the horses come in and the rough roping of the renegades. Fitz collected his party and pulled out first, the wagon jolting rather clumsily at the head of the procession. In another short while Seastrom had lined his prisoners out between the barracks; he himself trotted back to Charterhouse.

"Listen, don't expose yourself too much. Don't linger. Some of those fellows that flew the coop might come back to say by-by and have a shot at you. If I hear any such shots heaving across the prairie—"

"If you hear any such shots," interrupted Charterhouse harshly, "keep right on going. Don't come back."

Seastrom shifted in the saddle, softly swore and wheeled away. Charterhouse rose and crossed to the fire, kicking together the burning boards. A shower of hot sparks circled in the night. He watched them wink and vanish and then in slow weariness left the rim of light and settled on a barrack step. The rumor of the departing men died out, the smell of powder smoke faded in the air, and Fort Carson lay silent under the shadow of Dead Man's Ridge. There in the darkness, Clint rolled a cigarette and touched a match. The flare set off the stony triangle of his face, the cold flash of half-shut eyes—all the features drawn with suspense and grim unpleasantness. The match went out and he leaned back to hear the small sounds of night rise from the earth. His cigarette tip glowed and dimmed, but he held it so that no tell-tale light escaped the cup of his hand. Thus he waited, never stirring.

Nor did he move twenty-odd minutes later when the rhythmic advance of a rider sounded down the line of poplars, slacked and became a slow walk. Man and horse cut across the plaza. Steel glinted, and a tall form swayed to one side of the saddle. Charterhouse let a long, slow sigh escape him; this was the end, the climax, the tragic conclusion of Casabella's old story. Good men and bad men, strong men and weak men—Casabella took them all, touched them with its flame of unreason and tempted them to ruin through their weaknesses.

The tall form slipped from the saddle and came into the circle of light. A hand rose and tipped back the broad-brimmed hat. A fringe of yellow hair gleamed to the light. Buck Manners' bold, reckless face stared across the flame tips.

"I knew you'd come," drawled Charterhouse.

Manners started, whirled, and flung himself back again.
"Who is it?" he challenged.

"Charterhouse—waiting for you."

Manners' eyes flashed. He bulked larger, more formidable. "So? What the devil has been going on around here? I heard the shooting away off and rode like a condemned man. What happened? Good gosh, man, I have told you before I didn't believe in your policy. If you've brought on a fight—"

Charterhouse rose and came into the light. He tossed away the cigarette like a man come to a definite conclusion. "We'll omit all the preliminaries. You can drop the curtain, Manners. I saw behind it this morning up on the ridge when you rode down to meet Shander and the others."

Manners' face slowly hardened, slowly abandoned all the easy, reckless freedom. "You alone?" he muttered.

"I waited for you. The rest have gone. There's just one question puzzling me. Having all the chips you ever would need, what was your idea in dealing from the bottom of the deck?"

"Does it matter?"

"I wondered," replied Charterhouse, seeming sleepy. "My guess is you like to be the strong man, the top of the heap. I saw it at Angels when we muscled down."

"You're wise," droned Manners. "Too wise. You're the first to guess anywheres near right. But even you don't know what kind of hell fire and torture comes from a man's conscience."

"I can guess," said Charterhouse. "But only a fool would expect to keep his crooked trail secret."

"I chose my men well. Haggerty, Shander, Wolfert, Studd and Curly—they were the only ones who knew my part. The others never caught on. There isn't a man on my own outfit, nor a man on Box M, nor any other living soul in Casabella that knows. Unless you have told!"

"I keep my own counsel."

"I figured so. When I left Box M early this morning, before dawn, I knew you'd come on toward Carson to spy. I set Curly's men to drag the prairie and find you.

When they failed I knew there was just one thing left—let
you go through with your scheme of fighting. You overheard Curly's plan in Angels. You figured to have your
Box M men follow you up tonight and cut into Curly after dark. I knew that. There is nothing I don't know. So I
decided to let you go ahead."

"So I'd get a bullet and forget what I'd learned?" suggested Charterhouse. "Well, there was a sense in that.
Easier to catch a man by letting him go ahead with his
own idea than to chase him. I will admit you had me puzzled. All this horsing around the prairie left me some dubious. Didn't know if Curly was going through with his
original business or if he was going to cut behind me and
hit Box M. There was just one thing that turned the
scales, Manners. I'm giving you credit for one good quality. And that good quality tripped you."

"You knew I'd never let Curly attack the house Sherry
Nickum was in!" cried Manners.

"That turned the scales," admitted Charterhouse. "So I
hit back for Carson and waited. But I don't understand.
Knowing what you did know, why did you let me bait the
trap for Curly and Shander?"

Manners stood like a dragoon, magnificent body stiff
and square. The firelight darkened his cheeks and accent-
ed the brooding flame in his eyes. He seemed to be thinking out his answer and it came slowly. "Because they were
getting beyond my control. I wanted them destroyed."

"You succeeded," was Charterhouse's grim answer.
"They're destroyed. And so is Haggerty. Which leaves
Wolfert and Studd."

"Wolfert was killed in Angels at noon. I had him killed.
Studd—Studd will not talk, not if they put him in screws
and crack his bones. But he will go, too."

"And that," went on Charterhouse softly, "leaves me."

They stood silent, the licking fire between. Manners
lifted his chin. "I would rather die this minute than have
Sherry know the truth about me."

"Yet your orders killed her dad—and probably her
brother."

A spasm of pain came over Manners' face. "Didn't I

tell you," he cried, "I'm answering my conscience for all that? Listen, Charterhouse. You and I are alike. Both physically strong men. Both old in the game. Yet there you are and here I am. You ought to get down on your knees and thank God you weren't born with a kink like me."

"If you had wiped 'em all out, taken Box M, ruled the county, married the girl—you still couldn't have kept her from knowing about you, soon or late."

"I believed I could," muttered Manners. "I believed I could. Because I love her."

"No. There's a difference between you deeper than Red Draw. No man ever was born who could fool a woman."

"I would rather die than have her know," repeated Manners. "You understand the answer to that?"

"It's why I waited for you," said Charterhouse evenly.

"Then there is no need to delay longer. If you are killed, it shall be laid to the door of a Curly man. If I am killed, any story is good enough. Only I'll ask you as a gentleman to seal your knowledge of me forever."

"Agreed," was Charterhouse's laconic answer. "I am sorry I can't wish you luck."

"You're a cool one," said Manners. "How shall we settle the draw?"

"Suggest we back away from the fire to the rim of light."

Manners stared intently over the flames; he seemed to be trying to frame a last phrase but it never came out. So he took his cue from Charterhouse and slowly stepped to the rear. They halted on the edge of light, the flickering blaze between them.

"Can you see me?" asked Clint.

"Clear enough," muttered the ranchman, towering full length.

"And the signal—"

"I need no favor from you," retorted Manners. "I will wait your draw."

"Then," droned Charterhouse, "fire."

The night breeze scooped the flame tips into a red curling tongue that for the instant rose between them, shutting out sight. Through this crimson film the bullets passed and the roar ran away into the eerie corners of the fort, dying with a remote whisper. There was no more firing. The flames sank and Charterhouse, never stirring, saw a yellow hatless head cushioned against the earth as if asleep. In that solitary glance he knew all there was to be known. Nor did he tarry. He slipped back the gun and strode for the sheds, found his horse and swung away from Carson. With the outline of the poplars and building behind he spoke softly to the tired beast and set it to a stiff gallop.

"I have killed him," he said mechanically. "The man's dead. And Sherry loved him. Good or bad, she loved him. And never in a thousand years will she forget or forgive me."

He raced by the wagon with its four accompanying riders without a hail. All the way back he seemed detached from himself, numb of mind, scarcely conscious he owned a body. There was but one throbbing, clanging idea in his head: the job was done, Manners was dead, and the girl waited for his return. Charterhouse turned square with the beckoning ranch lights and galloped into the yard, finding Fitz already arrived. He got stiffly down and started for the porch.

"Fitz—will you throw my gear over my own horse?"

"Traveling's done for the night," grunted the puncher.

"Not for me, Fitz. Not tonight, or any other night, I reckon. Bring the black around. I'm going into the house, just for a minute."

He knocked at the door and heard Sherry's voice. Passing through, he saw her rising from a chair, some strange, bright glow of beauty spreading over those fine features. And the picture, the last he knew he should ever see, gripped him in the throat and tied his tongue. She was speaking swiftly, yet half of the words he never heard.

"—never again, Clint."

"No," he repeated, "never again, I reckon. Sherry, I have finished my chore. There is nothing more to do."

"I think," she said gravely, "there will always be something for you to do, Clint. And never anybody else quite able to do it but you."

The sound of her voice made pure melody. He gripped his hat between his big hands, pressing on. "You asked me to do what had to be done."

"You have, Clint."

"So," he muttered. "More. I must tell you—Buck Manners is dead at Fort Carson."

"Clint—"

"We matched guns, and he lost."

"But, Clint, he wasn't—"

"I had to come. No help for it, no choice. And after such a thing, there can't be any place on Box M for me. I am riding out, Sherry."

She was quite still, resting her body against the fireplace mantel, never letting her eyes turn from him, white cheeked and again with that look of tragedy on her face. It shook him, it made the room impossible to be in.

"Think of me as charitably as you can. And good-bye."

He hurried through the door. Fitz was just bringing up his horse. Clint sprang to the saddle. "So long, Fitz. Turn down my plate at the table. Tell the boys I admire 'em like brothers."

And he was away, never hearing Fitzgibbon's muttered curiosity. The black surged fresh beneath him and he drove south at a headlong gait, not knowing why the haste was necessary nor understanding when he would stop. The prairie took him, the air turned crisper and the remote stars gleamed down. He forgot the passage of time; he was hardly conscious of his destination until trees were about him and then he discovered a meadow with a cabin in it. Bowlus' place. He pulled himself out of the abyss of his thoughts to find himself mortally tired. He slid down, unsaddled and picketed the horse; going into the cabin, he stumbled to the bed and drew his saddle blanket over him. In that first moment of relaxation, he stared at the ceiling and summed up in slow, bitter words all that Casabella had done for him.

"I have had my fling. Now I can go back to work—and say good-bye to fine dreams." Then he was asleep.

When Clint woke, the fresh fine sun was pouring into Bowlus' window. He turned on the bunk and lifted himself suddenly. The door was open, as he had left it the night before. Sherry Nickum sat quietly on the steps, watching him with a small, wistful smile.

"I have been waiting for you to sleep it out," said she. "Now that you're up, I think I can find some coffee and bacon on the shelf. We will eat—for I haven't had time for breakfast either—and then we will ride home in the sun. You gave me no time to say anything last night. So I had one of the boys follow and find where you went. And here I am. Clint, there is a long time ahead of us for explaining and so we will do none of it now. But you can't run away from me. There isn't any border far enough removed I won't follow you across. You see, I happen to know how you feel and I have known it for some time. As for me, you have your answer, or I wouldn't be here."

A slow smile came over his face. "Last night, Sherry, I thought I was an old man waiting to die."

"I think I can change that, Clint. You have always been saddled with responsibilities. So I am saddling you with more. Come run Box M—and me."

More Westerns from SIGNET

- [ ] **TERROR IN EAGLE BASIN by Cliff Farrell.** Once the deadliest of lawmen, he'd turned his back on violence . . . but now he was forced to buckle on his guns again. (#Q6469—95¢)

- [ ] **THE DALTON GANG by Harold Preece.** The incredible true story of the notorious Dalton brothers—four renegade lawmen who declared war on the railroads and the banks in the West's last great reign of terror. (#Q6435—95¢)

- [ ] **THE LAST COMANCHERO by Ray Hogan.** Deep in the desert, Shawn Starbuck plays cat and mouse with the man who holds his brother captive—Valdez, leader of the Comancheros! (#Q6426—95¢)

- [ ] **BOUNTY MAN by Lewis B. Patten.** Tracking down two desperate murderers, Ross Dunbar stops on a mission of mercy and finds himself trapped instead! (#Q6366—95¢)

- [ ] **REURN OF THE LONG RIDERS by Cliff Farrell.** A tragic feud turned friendship into hate, violence, and murder! (#Q6323—95¢)

- [ ] **THE ORPHANS OF COYOTE CREEK by Lewis B. Patten.** Three spunky kids fight off a vicious killer in this new novel of the West by the Spur award-winning, bestselling author. (#Q6322—95¢)